W9-AXU-332

To Catch a Golden Ring

Marilyn Cram Donahue

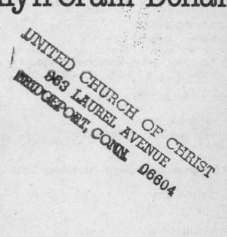
UNITED CHURCH OF CHRIST
963 LAUREL AVENUE
BRIDGEPORT, CONN. 06604

Chariot Books

To Trini
Who walks tall today

ACKNOWLEDGMENTS:
My special thanks to my dear friend Carol Reader, R.N., and to
Joan Keller, R.N., rehabilitation coordinator (both of San
Bernardino Community Hospital) for the generous sharing of their
time and for their invaluable technical information.

Chariot Books is an imprint of David C. Cook Publishing Co.

David C. Cook Publishing Co., Elgin, Illinois 60120
David C. Cook Publishing Co., Weston, Ontario

TO CATCH A GOLDEN RING
© 1980 by Marilyn Cram Donahue

All rights reserved. Except for brief excerpts for review purposes,
no part of this book may be reproduced or used in any form
without written permission from the publisher

Cover photo by Robert Cushman Hayes

Pennypincher edition, 1984
Printed in the United States of America
89 88 87 86 85   5 4 3 2

Library of Congress Cataloging in Publication Data

Donahue, Marilyn Cram.
  To catch a golden ring.

  "A Pennypincher book."
  Summary: Thirteen-year-old Angie is upset when she hears
another girl call the street where she lives a slum, then feels
responsible when her best friend loses his legs in an accident
while trying to escape from it.
  [1. Los Angeles (Calif.)—Fiction.   2. Physically
handicaped—Fiction] I. Title.
PZ7.D71475to 1984   [Fic]   80-68312
ISBN 0-89191-831-0

Contents

1
BUNDY STREET

Angie skated hard. It felt good to go fast. The cool air rushed past her, twisting her straight, brown hair into long tangles and drying the sweat inside her elbows and behind her ears.

It had been hot and horrible inside the roller rink. It was the first day of summer vacation, and everybody was supposed to be celebrating. But she was glad she had left.

Bundy Street was next. She was almost home.

"Angie! Wait for me."

She heard Con's voice, but she didn't slow down. Traitor! He'd stood right there and let stupid Jessica tell everybody that Bundy Street was a ...

"Angie! What's the matter with you?"

Con was right behind her, but Angie didn't turn her head. She coasted past Pete's Parking Lot, dodged Old Lu's flower cart on the corner, and skidded to a stop when the light turned red. She made a hard left turn and had already started down Bundy Street when she felt Con's hand on her arm.

Angie was tall for thirteen, and slim, like all the Raffertys. She was also strong, especially when she was mad. But Con was bigger and stronger. He reached out and whirled her around in a half circle until she was facing the other way; then he stopped her short.

"What are you trying to prove?"

"I was in a hurry." Angie spoke the next words very slowly, through her teeth. "I still am."

"Look, Angie. You don't have to be mad at me. I'm not the one who said we live in a slum."

She put both hands over her ears. "Don't say that word to me. It's a lie. Why didn't you stand up and call Jessica a liar?"

Con raised both eyebrows. "You were doing a pretty good job of that. Anyway, it doesn't do any good to start an argument with someone like Jessica. She likes to put people down."

Angie shook her head. "Bundy Street is where we live. Nobody should call it Slumsville."

Con looked down the street. "It's where we live all right." Then he lifted one shoulder and let it drop in a shrug. "I guess we're used to it."

"What do you mean by that?"

She hated it when people said only half of what they were thinking. Con did it all the time. He was her best friend, but sometimes she couldn't figure him out.

He was staring down the street. The skin between his eyebrows made a deep question mark.

She looked down the length of the street, too, trying to figure out what he was seeing. Everything looked just the same as it always did. She closed her eyes and sniffed. It smelled the same, too. When you stood at this end of the street, you could always get a whiff of the popcorn from the Mayan Theater.

A siren whooped, pounding the air with a steady beat, and car horns played a staccato rhythm against the low roar of engines. From two doors down came the unmistakable smell of hot pastrami and the sound of Tony Genovese's hand organ. Tony ran the Deli seven days a week, but on Saturday night he took his monkey to Chinatown and played for pennies. Tony Genovese was one of the last of the hurdy-gurdy men.

6

Angie smiled. People like Tony didn't live in slums.

She nudged Con. "What's eating you, anyway?"

He turned and looked at her. For a second, the sunlight was on his face, and she could count the freckles.

"Nothing's the matter," he told her. "It's just that ... I guess when you look at the same things every day, you really don't see them anymore."

There he went again. Angie's other friends talked about each other. Con was the only person she knew who talked about thoughts. It made her feel uncomfortable, as if somebody was about to pull a rug out from under her.

"Don't be silly," she snapped. "I can tell you anything you want to know about this place, and I look at it every day."

Con shook his head. "That's not what I mean. You look at things, but do you really see them?"

He left the question hanging between them and turned away, skating slowly along the broken sidewalk.

"I don't know what you're talking about," she said to his back. But she did know. Deep in her throat, she felt a tiny bubble of understanding. She caught up with him and matched her rhythm with his. She didn't intend to talk about it anymore.

But Con wasn't through. He skated past Tony's and pointed to the stucco front of the Universal Mission. "Just look at that!"

Angie saw the cracked, yellowed glass set high under the roof in six square windows. In between the windows was a larger-than-life figure of what seemed to be George Washington, covered with gold paint. He was standing on top of a metal frame that held neon letters spelling: PRAYER CHANGES THINGS.

Propped against the closed double doors sat a fully clothed sunbather, apparently asleep. Along the front of the mission, pieces of stucco had chipped away and exposed irregular patches of red brick siding.

Angie shrugged. "It looks just like it did yesterday."

"That's right. And I'll bet your eyesight was just as bad then as it is now." Con lowered his voice. "Can't you be honest, Angie? Can't you try to see things the way they really are?"

Angie stared at him until her eyes blurred. Then she knelt quickly and loosened one skate. She took her time pulling the lace up tight, waiting until she didn't have to blink anymore.

She knew Con was waiting for her, but she got up slowly and brushed the dusty knee of her jeans. She wasn't going to look at him.

"Hey," he said. "I'm sorry. Listen. Angie ..."

Angie looked straight ahead and started to skate. When she felt Con reach for her hand and squeeze it, she didn't pull away, but she didn't look at him either. They passed Corky's, Customer Parking Only, and waited at the corner for the light to change.

Con's words were in her head, louder than when he had spoken them.

Can't you be honest, Angie? Can't you try to see things the way they really are?

Did that mean seeing them with Jessica's eyes? Angie looked across at Chico's Cabin. It was made of logs, painted bright red. Gray barbecue smoke was coming out of a chimney on the back.

On the other side of the driveway called Chico's Alley stood Hoang Chou's Laundry. There was a tiny label on the door that said so. But the large black letters across the upper floor—where Hoang Chou lived with his wife, Amy, and eight kids—said West Coast Desk Company.

"But what about all the ones who are looking for a laundry?" Angie had asked.

Hoang Chou had grinned, "They can smell that."

It was true. The steamy wet vapor seeped through

the walls of the old building. What Hoang Chou didn't know was that it didn't go very far before it smelled like the rest of the street: a deep city fragrance. A mixture of hot tortillas, barbecue smoke, popcorn, pastrami, dusty asphalt, exhaust fumes, and carnations from Old Lu's cart.

The old green building where Angie and Con lived was next. It had one front door, like ordinary houses, but inside it was divided up the middle by a narrow stairway, which stretched like an open accordion to the second floor. There were four apartments on the bottom, two on each side of the stairs. The second floor was identical.

The eight front steps of the apartment were flanked by four skinny white columns, which had once decorated the side door of Morrison's Funeral Home.

The light changed, and Angie skated across the street. The barbecue smell from Chico's made her stomach growl. She glanced at the picnic table in the alley. It was covered with food scraps and black flies.

Angie supposed her sister Caro was getting hungry by now. "My mother's going to kill me," she told Con.

"Why? You're not late, are you?"

"I ... didn't tell her I was going." She could feel Con looking at her. "She wouldn't have let me."

They reached the house and clumped noisily up the wooden steps. He put his hand on the doorknob. "I hope it was worth it," he said.

Then he opened the door. The hall was dark and smelled like stale bread. But it wasn't quiet. Inner doors slammed, like echoes behind the walls. A telephone rang, and rang again. Mrs. Marenga, from upstairs, was singing in her low gypsy voice. Water gurgled in the pipes ... was silent ... then gurgled again. From Angie's apartment (to the right of the front door) came the sound of broken glass, then gunshots and a siren.

Angie bent and unlaced her skates. The broken glass

was probably real. The rest was television.

Con already had his skates in his hand. He grinned and put one finger on the tip of Angie's nose. It was a kind of secret thing between them. It meant "I'm OK ... you're OK." Their signal for a smile.

But Angie didn't feel like smiling.

"Come on, Angie!" He waited.

Lately Con had seemed like more than her best friend. She didn't always understand him, but she would do anything in the world for him. She knew he felt the same way.

Angie smiled.

"That's better. Hey! Do you have to baby-sit?"

"Probably." Her mother worked weekends whenever she could. Tips were good at Corky's on weekends.

"How about popping some popcorn? We could take it up on the roof."

Angie hesitated. "Caro would have to come, too."

"So what? She's a good kid. Anyway, I want to get out tonight."

Angie knew why. Con had a new stepfather. He'd had several, and this was the worst of the bunch. It wasn't because he was out of work most of the time. It was because he was just plain mean.

"Why don't you eat dinner with us?" she asked. She knew her mother wouldn't mind. She liked Con, and Angie was the one who did the cooking anyway.

Con looked relieved. "I thought you'd never ask. I'll get rid of my skates and be back in a second."

He climbed the stairs two at a time. Angie knew he didn't have to ask permission. His mother wasn't the kind to worry. "Con is fifteen," she would say. "He can take care of himself."

Angie moved toward her own door. Her mother said they were lucky to live at the front of the house. The apartments were larger there, and you could see up and down Bundy Street from the kitchen window.

The door opened before Angie had a chance to turn the key in the lock.

"Where have you been?" Her mother's face looked as tight as Angie's felt when she pulled her hair back hard and fastened it with a rubber band.

"There was a skating party. It's the first day of vacation. I didn't think you'd mind."

That wasn't true. She knew her mother would mind. How could she go to work if Angie wasn't there to take care of Caro?

"We have rules in this house, young lady!"

Angie looked at the floor. "I'm sorry if I worried you."

"You didn't!" Her mother was very white. "But you made me late for work. I could lose my job!

"I'm working extra hours, Angie, so we can get out of here someday. Do you want to live on Bundy Street for the rest of your life?" She closed the door quietly behind her, but Angie felt as if she had slammed it hard.

Bundy Street! Bundy Street! Was that all anybody could talk about? Angie waited until she was sure her mother was gone; then she went to the front door, opened it, and stepped out onto the bright green porch.

The sun was setting, and the western sky was streaked with crimson cloud trails. Angie had seen it at sunset a hundred times, but today she made herself look at it hard.

Old Lu was pushing her flower cart across the street. Nobody knew where she went at night. She just disappeared until morning.

The Deli was a dark spot between the brightness of the Mayan Theater and the flashing neon sign of the mission.

This was Bundy Street. This was where she lived.

2
CAROUSEL

The roof was like a big flat porch. It was Angie's favorite place on a clear night.

"What are you so mad about?" Caro stuffed a handful of popcorn into her mouth and stared at Angie, waiting for an answer. Con rolled over on his stomach and reached for an apple.

"She's not mad. She's just thinking."

"About what?"

"About living here."

"Oh ... What's there to think about? It's a dump. As soon as I get old enough, I'm leaving."

Angie had to hand it to Caro. She was only ten years old, but she faced facts.

Angie plopped down on one of the big pillows that they'd found in the empty room on the third floor.

"How old do you think is old enough?" Angie asked.

"As old as you are," Caro said. "Three years to go for me. Look at it this way. If you don't get out of here while you can, you never will. You'll be trapped, like mom. I'll bet she'd run, if she could. But she's got us."

Caro reached for an apple and took a bite. "I don't know what's keeping you two." She looked at Con. "Especially you."

He reached over and pulled her red hair. "Running away isn't always the answer. Haven't you ever heard of the truant officer?"

"Hah!" Caro made a face. "Haven't you ever heard of staying out of sight?" She got up and took the rest of the popcorn with her. "I'm going downstairs to watch television."

Con stood up so suddenly he looked like he had been pulled up by a string through the top of his head.

"How can you do that?" Angie asked him.

"Leg muscles. From swimming, I guess." He laughed. "I haven't got wings, Angie, but I can go almost anywhere on these legs."

It was probably true. Con could run and jump and swim like nobody she'd ever seen. He had only started high school this year, and the coach was already talking about varsity teams.

He stretched his arms high, as if he was reaching for the crescent moon that hung between two stars. "If I could fly, that's where I'd go. I'd hang from the moon and swing like a monkey."

"But you can't fly, Con. Nothing flies around here. Not even real-for-sure flies," Angie suddenly felt heavy, as if she weighed one thousand pounds. "It's all your fault."

Con looked surprised.

"You know what I mean. You told me to take a good look at Bundy Street. Well, I did, and I wish I hadn't. I felt better when I was mad at Jessica."

"Come on, Angie. Pretty soon you're going to sound like Caro."

"She's not so dumb."

"She's not so smart, either. She talks big to hide the way she really feels. Look, if you ran away, where would you go?"

"Someplace where I could get a job." Angie shivered. It was getting cold out here.

"At thirteen? You're nuts."

He was right, but she wasn't going to say so. She stood up. "I have to check on Caro."

"No you don't. You want to change the subject."

She wasn't going to listen. She went to an opening at the edge of the roof and climbed down the metal ladder that led to a narrow balcony at the back of the house. Then she opened the door into the empty room on the third floor. She tossed the pillows into a corner and kept right on going. Her feet beat a syncopated rhythm on the steps.

Con was right behind her. He was still talking. "Look, Angie, just because you face facts, you don't have to let the truth get you down."

She looked over her shoulder. "What do you expect me to do? Celebrate?"

He shook his head. "You have to have a plan. You can stand almost anything if you have a plan."

"Such as …?"

Con smiled. "When you feel like you're going around in circles, enjoy the ride."

Angie squinted. "I think you really are crazy."

"Probably. Can you get out of here by ten tomorrow morning?"

"Maybe. What for?"

"Don't you have any imagination, girl? To enjoy the ride!"

Con took the stairs three at a time and stood at the top, laughing. He knew she couldn't stand a secret. Angie opened her apartment door and slammed it shut behind her.

"Enjoy your own ride," she muttered. But she knew she would be ready by ten. Wherever he was going, she wasn't going to be left behind.

She was ready before ten. She slipped early into the tiny kitchen off the living room and stirred some powdered milk into a glass of water. She lit the gas burner with a match. Then she stuck a long-handled fork into a piece of bread and toasted it over the open fire.

She had to move like a cat. This place was so small and old, one squeak would wake everybody. She and

Caro slept together in a bed that dropped down out of the living room wall. At one time a painted panel of wood had covered the bottom of the bed. But the panel had split, and now there was just a flowered curtain stretched across the top and bottom of the springs to keep them from showing.

Angie sighed and chewed her toast. She put her glass in the sink and tiptoed back into the living room and through the door into the narrow hall that led to the bathroom and her mother's room.

She stood outside her mother's door, trying to breathe without making any noise. Her clothes were in there. There was only one closet in the house.

She took six steps across the room. Opened the closet door. Found clean jeans and a T-shirt.

"What are you looking for?"

Angie dropped everything. Her mother was sitting up in bed, watching her.

"My clothes." Angie might as well tell the truth. "Con wants me to go somewhere."

"Well, go on. Just let me sleep."

"Hey ... mom?"

"What is it?"

"I was going to leave you a note."

"Sure you were!" Her mother sighed. "OK, OK, I believe you. Have a good time." She fell back against the pillow. "Angle ...?"

"Yeah?"

"Try to be home by four? I'll fix dinner tonight. But I really can't be late for work again."

"Sure, mom."

Angie pulled on her clothes and walked carefully across the living room. Caro turned over and groaned. Too much popcorn. Served her right.

Angie smiled to herself. They weren't too bad, her family. Better than Con's. She ran outside to wait.

When Con wasn't there, she leaned against one of

the pillars and scuffed at a stray weed with her shoe. She'd noticed it a few days ago, growing right out of a crack in the concrete and climbing up the side of the steps like a vine.

She heard voices upstairs, left front. That was Con's apartment. His stepfather was talking loud, but the words jumbled, and Angie couldn't make out what he was saying. She could hear Con.

"This place is crowded, all right. It was full before, but now it's crowded!"

Then the window slammed, and she couldn't hear any more. Poor Con. It must be awful to have a stepfather who yelled at you all the time.

Angie's own father had left when Caro was a baby. He had to go away. Their mother said so, and then she wouldn't talk about it anymore.

Angie tried and tried, but she couldn't remember what he looked like. She liked to pretend that he had just gone away for a while, like the father in *Little Women*. He might walk in the front door any day. She knew the way it would be; she had rehearsed the scene a thousand times in her mind.

He would be singing as he came down the street. He'd have a huge voice, like Tony Genovese's.

He would stop singing and whistle a little as he came up the steps. Angie could see the shape of him clearly in her mind. He'd hold the black railing in one hand. His head would be high, and under his arm would be a long box—red roses for her mother.

He'd have something for Angie, too. In his pocket, in a blue velvet jeweler's box with a snap-top lid. It would be a golden ring with miniature flowers carved into its surface and Angie's full name—Angelina—etched in tiny, delicate letters.

Angie would be the only one home when he arrived. That was the way she imagined it. She would walk to the door and stand there with her heart beating hard.

16

Then she would reach out and turn the knob. The door would open, and she'd hold out her arms. She'd feel herself lifted in the air and swung round and round until she was dizzy.

But no matter how hard she tried, she never saw his face.

"Angie! What's the matter with you?"

Angie blinked rapidly. It was Con. "I ... guess I was daydreaming."

"You sure were. You were a million miles away."

His voice was hoarse. Angie looked at his face and wondered what had happened upstairs.

"Well, I'm back now," she said. "Where's this ride we're supposed to enjoy?"

Con took her by the hand and started off at a run down Bundy Street. They arrived at Chico's corner just before the number 15 bus did. It paused just long enough for Con to pull Angie on behind him and drop his coins in the slot. Then it jolted, hissed, and inched forward as the light turned green.

"We're going on a *bus* ride?"

"Temporarily. Then we have to walk."

That was evidently all he was going to tell her. Angie sat back and looked out the window. She'd never been on the number 15 bus. The sign in the window said La Mirada. That would mean La Mirada Beach. She'd been to the ocean a few times, but not to La Mirada.

It was a long twenty minutes, full of sidewalk scenery and brief, jolting stops. Angie noticed that all the cross streets had numbered names—Fifteenth, Fourteenth, Thirteenth—and the numbers were getting smaller and smaller with every block. When they reached Third Street, Con pulled the cord and stood up.

"This is it. We walk from here."

They were at the top of a hill. The sidewalk descended like a curving pathway, past small cottages.

17

The sun was hot on Angie's back as they started down the hill, but a fresh wind cooled her face and blew her hair back. She saw the ocean ahead, deep blue and sprinkled with white foam.

"Where are we going?"

Con pointed, "Straight ahead."

Straight ahead was the ocean. A little to the left, a large pier rose high above the sand and stretched out across the water. Children were playing on the shady beach beneath it, and farther out fishermen were casting their lines into the sea. But the pier looked like an amusement park on the water.

Angie followed Con up the steep cement steps to the top of the pier and looked around. Brightly painted booths were filled with souvenirs: stuffed animals, fancy hats, even goldfish in bowls. Carnival music was punctuated with the *Pop! Pop!* of target guns. Laughter rose and fell with the sound of the surf.

Con was pulling her by the hand towards a red ticket booth with a glass top. A golden sunburst covered the front, with sea nymphs dancing in its rays. Painted on the front window was the word *TICKETS* in fancy letters.

Con put some coins on the counter and picked up two yellow tickets. "Come on!"

He put both hands on her shoulders and turned her around until she was facing the big red building behind the ticket booth. The sign above the entrance spelled C-A-R-O-U-S-E-L in red letters lined with gold.

All around the building were dozens of tall, narrow doorways that led inside. There was an upper level where mullioned windows shown in the sunlight like bright eyes and where four square towers sat on each corner like guards. The metal roof sloped upward like a great silver cap gleaming in the sunlight. Angie's breath caught in her throat.

The crowd surged forward, and Angie stumbled through the turnstile. She stood with Con at a wooden railing where people were waiting to go in. An enclosed balcony with windows in it ran around the upper walls of the big room. Angie wished she were up there where she could watch instead of down here where it was all happening.

The carousel slowed down and stopped. The gate opened, and Angie felt herself pushed forward by the crowd behind her. The music she had heard outside began again, slowly at first, then faster, until the room was filled with a sound like a thousand hand organs.

Wide-eyed horses held their heads high. Painted manes tossed wildly. Faster and faster ... round and round ... up and down.

"Pick a horse, Angie. This is the only place in the world where you can go in circles and enjoy the ride."

As if at his signal, the merry-go-round slowed and stopped. Con pulled her to the platform and helped her onto a pink horse.

Angie's stomach did a quick flop, and she held the brass pole tightly with both hands. Con climbed onto the horse next to hers. Then he leaned over and pulled her seat belt tight. She wondered what it would feel like when the carousel turned. She hoped she wasn't going to be sick.

"Hey, Angie ..."

She looked at Con and knew he must have read her mind. He reached over and loosened her fingers. "You don't have to hold on so tight. If you reach out your hand, you might even catch a golden ring."

3
A PERFECT DAY

Golden ring? Angie shot a question at him with her eyes. He gave her a freckled grin; then he pointed to a contraption attached to the wall of the building. It stuck out like a horizontal metal arm with a shiny silver loop at the tip.

"But that's a silver ring," Angie said.

"It sure is. Only a few are gold. Brass, really. Every time you ride by, you're supposed to lean way out and reach for one. If one is gold, you get a free ride."

"How far out is way out?"

Con grasped the pole with his left hand, put his weight on the right stirrup, and leaned out as far as he could stretch his right arm.

The music started, and she felt her horse quiver. Suddenly, Con unbuckled his belt, slid from his horse, and climbed quickly onto the one in front of Angie. Then he twisted around and looked at her.

"Watch me," he ordered. "Do just what I do."

The platform was really moving now, faster and faster. To Angie's horror her horse was moving, too. Up and down. Up and down. She tried to smile, but her mouth belonged to somebody else. The music filled her head, louder and faster, bells and chimes and organ sounds all mixed together and about to explode under the canopy of bright lights.

Gradually she felt herself relax with the movement and the music, and daring to hold the brass pole with only one hand, she reached out and ran her other fingers over the pink horse's head.

Con twisted around so he could see her. "Now, watch me!" he ordered.

He stood, his weight on his right foot, waiting. When they passed the ring machine, he stretched out his arm, hooked a finger into the loop, and pulled. A silver circle came away free; and another popped immediately into its place.

The next ring came into view. Con took it and waved his hand triumphantly. Two bright silver circles now dangled on his finger.

The carousel turned full circle, and Con claimed a third ring. "Silver again," he complained.

Angie reached for the next one and missed. Her fingers didn't even touch it. On the next try, she felt a quick brush of metal against her fingertips. She was getting closer. Next time, she leaned as far as she could without falling out of the saddle. She touched the loop, caught it with her index finger, and felt it slip away.

"I don't think your arms are long enough," Con teased. He reached out in front of her and snapped off a ring. He had a handful now—all silver.

She was right behind him, but there wasn't much time left. She stood all the way up. Her finger was in the loop. She closed her eyes and pulled.

It all happened in an instant. "Look!" she cried to Con. Only when she opened her hand to show him did she realize that the ring she held was gold.

"Beginner's luck!" he exclaimed.

But Angie knew he was as excited as she was. He slipped from his horse and helped her down. His hands stayed around her waist for a second, and he stood smiling down at her.

"Do you want your free ride now?" he asked.

Angie shook her head. "Let's wait a while." Her legs felt wobbly, like she'd been riding a real horse.

Angie stuffed it deep into the pocket of her jeans and followed Con through the exit and onto the pier. It smelled different than Bundy Street here. Mostly, it was the salt. It penetrated everything. Even the hamburgers cooking on a hot grill smelled a little of the sea.

She and Con walked to the railing and leaned against the rusty metal, looking over the side to the water below.

"It's a long way down there," Angie said.

"It's a long way *out* there." Con swung his arm across the horizon. "That's where I want to go, Angie. It's a big world, and I want to see it."

Angie felt the gold ring in her pocket. Too bad it wasn't a magic carpet. "You're forgetting something," she said aloud. "We're stuck on Bundy Street."

Con put his arm around her shoulders, squeezed her hard, and laughed.

"That's only temporary," he told her. "Remember what I told you about having a plan? I'm not going to be on Bundy Street forever, and neither are you. Listen, Angie, Mr. Erickson at school says I have a pretty good chance of getting an athletic scholarship for college. What do you think of that?"

She stared hard at a large pigeon. It hopped along the railing, stretching its iridescent green neck in the sunlight. Angie flapped her hands vigorously. *You can go wherever you want, so go on and go,* she said to herself as she watched the pigeon.

"Well, what do you think?" Con was asking. "Hey, Angie. What's the matter?"

He leaned over and looked into her face; then he sighed. "You never listen to a thing I say, do you?"

"I'm listening now."

He sighed again. He looked at her, she thought, as if

she were not very bright. So what? She didn't feel very bright. Con would get a scholarship and go away. Then she'd probably die, and they'd bury her on Bundy Street.

"You're a smart girl, Angie. But sometimes you can't see what's under your nose. Do you think I'd make a plan that didn't include you? You're a better student than I am anyway. You won't have any trouble getting a scholarship yourself, an academic one at that. Sure, you'll be a year or two behind me, but ..."

He put out one hand and touched hers. "That just gives me time to pave the road. Look, Angie. Don't you see? School is our ticket out of Bundy Street. I know we can do it—the two of us together. But it has to be our plan, not *mine*."

Angie couldn't look at him. "I thought—"

"I know what you thought. You're pretty dumb sometimes." He gave her a gentle poke. "Come on."

They walked past booth after booth, all packed together with common walls, so that the noises and smells from one leaked over into all the others. Hot dogs, hamburgers, pink cotton candy, saltwater taffy—even French fried potatoes in paper containers with catsup dribbled over the top.

Angie took a deep breath and let it out slowly. She wished she could stay here at the beach forever.

Then she heard the sound of a boy coughing. She'd heard that cough before. It sounded just like his voice—high and kind of whining.

Then she heard him speak. "Hey, Howard, what're you doin' here?"

Con's real name was Howard. Howard Conway. But Angie only knew one person who called him that. Took.

Con looked at Angie, and the name passed, unspoken, between them. Why did Took always have to show up where he wasn't wanted? He was like a black cat, Angie thought. He crossed your path and brought

23

you bad luck.

She turned around and saw him. He had his thumbs hooked into the loops on his pants where a belt should have been. He always stood like that, and he always had a bad cold. Angie didn't know why Con put up with him.

"Hey, Howie," Took was saying. "How about some surfing? The waves are good, and a lotta the guys are down there."

Angie wondered how much trouble she would get into if she backed him up to the rail and pushed him over into the ocean. She had just about decided it would be worth the risk when Con reached out and thumped Took on the back.

It was a friendly thump, and Con's voice was friendly, too. "Not today, Took. Thanks, anyway."

Angie watched with amazement as she realized what Con was doing. He was turning Took around and starting him off in the opposite direction.

"You go ahead," Con said, "and we'll see you later." He waved his hand.

"I can't stand him. He's like a—"

"I know. But he can't help it. It's all a put-on. He tries to act important, because he doesn't have anything to act important about."

Angie shrugged. "Who cares about Took?"

He gave her a quick look. "That's just what I mean. Nobody cares. Took could disappear tomorrow, and he probably wouldn't even become a missing person."

Con sighed. He did that sometimes when he was about to say something he'd thought a lot about. "Do you know why Took is an outsider, Angie?"

She could think of about a million reasons. She opened her mouth, but Con kept on talking.

"It's because we keep him outside. We don't try to understand what makes him the way he is."

24

Angie sniffed. She didn't want to understand Took. She didn't even want to talk about him anymore. "He's not my responsibility," she said.

"Maybe he's not," he told her. "But don't be too sure. Sometimes we don't get to choose our responsibilities. They just fall into our laps."

Angie looked at him sideways. She wasn't about to ruin this day with an argument, so she kept her mouth shut. But she knew one thing for sure. Never, in her whole life, did she intend to take any responsibility for Took.

The music came so softly at first that Angie wasn't sure she even heard it. "Tony!" she exclaimed. "What's Tony doing here?"

Tony Genovese, his monkey, and Tony's hurdy-gurdy machine were coming toward them. All the Genoveses had been organ grinders. Hurdy-gurdy men, Tony liked to call them. They used to make their livings with their hand organs and little monkeys; but times had changed, and now the Deli paid Tony's bills. His hand organ was saved for weekends.

It was a beautiful old-timer, made of dark, polished wood and painted with a border of yellow roses. Tony said it had been in his family for more than a hundred years. It reminded Angie of a giant music box, set in a cart on wheels.

Right now Bandit was on the outside, perched on top of the organ, where he could stretch his tiny neck and look around. Tony stopped in the middle of the wharf, dangled Bandit's leather rope in one hand, and began turning the crank with the other.

The music came out, loud and clear. Angie loved it. It was happy music. It made her feel gypsy free. When she listened to Tony, she didn't live on Bundy Street. She was a whisper on the wind.

The sound was a kind of signal to Bandit, too. He wrapped his tail around Tony's arm and swung, land-

Property of
United Church of Christ
Bridgeport, CT
203-368-3658

25

ing with a light-footed hop on the ground.

Tony held the rope lightly in one hand and manipulated it with his fingers. With the other hand Tony turned the crank of the organ.

Angie loved it when Bandit decided to do things his own way. He somersaulted and cavorted, putting pennies under his hat instead of into his pocket. Tony let him do it, laughing with the crowd, and only using the rope to keep Bandit from straying too far away.

The music stopped, and Bandit sprang to the top of the organ.

Con waved. "Tony! What're you doing here?"

Tony gave them a smile. "Chinatown on Saturday nights isn't enough to keep Bandit happy. This summer we decided to tackle La Mirada on Sunday afternoons. So, what've you kids been up to?"

Con laughed. "I'm showing Angie how to go around in circles and enjoy the ride. Show him, Angie."

Angie reached in her pocket and pulled out the golden ring. "Con says it's just beginner's luck. What do you think, Tony?"

Tony took off the little hat he wore with the yellow feather in the side. "Could be," he said.

Angie put the ring away and leaned back against the bench, letting the sun warm her all the way through. The salt air brushed against her skin, fanning her face and cooling the heat prickles on her arms and legs. It carried with it the distinct odor of corn dogs.

"This is the life," she said.

She felt Tony looking at her. "For a while," he agreed. "Everybody needs to take a break. But then it's time to get back to doing whatever it is you do." He got up and brushed off his pants. "This organ will get rusty if I don't make it sing."

They walked slowly out to the very end of the pier, where the Bait and Tackle Shop hung over the wooden steps that led down to the fishing barges and a little restaurant below. Con went to the open window and bought two frozen bananas. The chocolate covering was bitter and good, and it lasted all the way back to the beginning of the pier.

Con took Angie by the hand, and they walked to the sidewalk and started the climb to the bus stop at the top of the hill.

They sat by an open window on the bus so they could feel the wind. It was fun, looking out and counting off the streets, with nothing else to do.

The bus squealed its brakes and pulled to the curb. Angie didn't even remember getting off. But the next thing she knew they were at the front steps of the apartment house.

Con opened the door for her; then he touched her face with his fingertips.

She looked up at him and smiled. "It was a perfect day," she said, softly.

"Con!" It was a man's voice. Loud. And harsh.

Angie looked up to the top of the stairs. Orly, Con's stepfather, stood, holding onto the rail for balance with both hands. He was a big man, but he seemed larger than ever standing above them like that. The way he looked at them made Angie shiver. She suddenly felt as if she had been caught doing something wrong.

Con didn't look at her. "Go on inside, Angie."

She seemed to be moving in slow motion, backing toward her door, fumbling in her pocket for the key. She found it and twisted it in the lock.

"I'm waiting for you, Con." The voice was louder.

Angie stood with her back to the door. She seemed to have lost her voice. *Don't go up the stairs, Con. Go anywhere, but not up there. Run!*

Con's face had turned very white. Angie held her breath as he started climbing the stairs. She watched until he reached the top. Orly smiled at him, then moved back and made a mock bow, sweeping one arm out with the palm spread forward.

"After you," he said.

She swallowed hard. Why was Orly so angry? Con hadn't done anything wrong, unless ... Could Orly have found out that Con was hiding some of the money he earned?

Con walked past his stepfather, around the corner of the landing, and out of sight. Orly stayed there, looking at Angie.

He was still smiling. Then, just as if he had clicked a shutter, the picture changed and his face went hard. He leaned over the banister.

"Where've you kids been?" he whispered. "What've you been up to?"

Angie still couldn't speak. She wanted to tell him they hadn't been up to anything. She wanted to beg him not to hurt Con. But she just stood there and stared back at him.

"I'll get you," he told her. "One of these days, when you're not looking, I'll find a way to get you."

Angie didn't hesitate. Without another thought she slipped into the apartment and locked the door behind her. She stood, leaning with her back against it, waiting for her heart to stop thumping.

What had they been up to? Orly could make you feel wicked just by looking at you.

Angie closed her eyes and saw Orly standing at the top of the stairs, bowing to Con. She heard him saying, "I'll get you. One of these days ..." But she was safe behind a locked door, while Con was ...

Oh, be careful, Con. Give him your money if he wants it. Just be careful.

4
SOLITAIRE

"Hey, Angie. Where have you been?"

Caro was sitting at the card table.

"Where's mom?" Angie asked.

"Gone to work. She got called in early."

"Don't worry," Caro went on. "She wasn't mad. But she said you'd have to cook dinner after all."

Angie started to walk past Caro into the kitchen, but a loud noise stopped her. A noise like a piece of furniture falling.

Caro's head jerked up. When she spoke, her voice was too loud and too fast. "Mom said if anything happened, you were to stay inside. She said you were to turn on the television loud and lock the door." She grabbed Angie's arm. "Mom really meant it, because ... Orly's been looking for Con all afternoon."

Angie didn't stay inside. She unlocked the door and ran out into the hall.

"Angie, don't!"

She turned her head and looked back at Caro. Caro's face was white, and she was shaking all over. "If ... he gets you, Angie ... then he'll get me, too."

Angie sat down hard on the stairs. She was shaking almost as hard as Caro was.

But Con, how was she going to help Con? Her throat tightened until she could hardly breathe. It wasn't right

29

to sit and listen while someone you loved was ...

A loud shout from the apartment above made her jump. It was Con's voice, and it was followed by a low moan. Angie put her hands over her ears, but she couldn't stop the sounds. The apartment door flew open—she could hear it bang against the inside wall—and then the voices were louder than ever.

"What are you trying to prove?" Con's voice was strained, as if he didn't have any breath.

"I'm the boss around here. That's what I'm proving. From now on things are gonna go my way." There was a terrible crash, then several heavy thuds, like something was being banged against the wall, and the sound of struggling, as if Con was trying to push Orly away. Angie got up slowly and held on to the railing. She could hear Orly's voice.

"Look at me, boy! You're gonna quit school and go to work full time. ... And all the money comes to me."

"That's not fair—" Con, began.

But Orly just kept on yelling. "The second thing you're gonna do is stay away from that girl."

"Listen, Orly. Leave ... Angie out of this." Con's words were slow and forced as if he could hardly talk. "You can't stop me from being with Angie."

"Oh, can't I? You just try me and see. You like her, don't you? You wouldn't want to see her hurt, would you?"

Angie started backing slowly toward their door. Orly meant what he'd said. He would get her. She didn't know how, but she was sure he would think of a way.

The upstairs door slammed shut, and she couldn't hear their voices anymore. She pushed Caro ahead of her into the apartment, and they stood there looking at each other and waiting.

There was another loud crash from upstairs, then another and another. Angie couldn't stand it. "We've go to do something," she said, and was ashamed at the fear that showed in her voice.

Angie listened. It was quiet. A door slammed, and heavy footsteps thudded on the stairs. The front screen squeaked and banged.

"Quick!" Angie started for the kitchen window, but Caro was there first.

"It's Orly," she announced. "He's leaving."

Angie didn't wait another second. She unlocked the door and went up the stairs two at a time.

"Con!" she called, pounding on 2A. "Open the door. Are you all right, Con?"

The door opened a crack. It wasn't Con. Bernice looked through the slit. Bernice was Con's mother, and everybody called her by her first name because it was so hard to keep track of her last names.

"I … just wanted to know … that is, I heard … is … Con all right?"

"He'll be all right." Bernice began to close the door.

"Could I see him?"

"No! Go back downstairs. Leave us alone."

Angie had the terrible feeling that if she didn't see Con now she never would. "Please," she said.

"Go away. If it hadn't been for you, none of this would have happened."

The door slammed. Angie stood in the upstairs hallway for a long minute.

Con was hurt, and it was her fault. How was it her fault? She went over and over Bernice's words in her mind, trying to digest them by repetition. Bernice's words didn't make any sense at all.

"Bernice is absolutely crazy!"

Saying the words out loud made Angie feel better. She hadn't done anything bad. She'd gone to the beach, and she'd come home, and she'd stood at the bottom of the stairs, talking to Con.

Maybe that was it. Maybe Orly didn't want anyone taking Con's time. If it hadn't been for Angie, Con might not have wanted to go to the beach and spend the money Orly wanted.

Caro was waiting in the doorway. "Who are you talking to? Did you see Con?"

Angie ignored the first question and answered the second. "I saw Bernice. She wouldn't let me in. She said Con will be all right."

Caro made a noise like a horse's whinny. "Bernice is stupid. I wouldn't take her word for anything. You ought to go and talk to Tony."

Sometimes Angie could hardly believe that Caro was only ten years old. Of course. Tony was the obvious person to talk to. He was the only one on the block who wasn't afraid of Orly. Bernice would let Tony in, and he wouldn't leave until she had told him the whole truth.

"Look," Angie said, "I'm not going to leave you here alone. We'll both go and wait for Tony."

"Isn't he home?"

"He's at the beach. La Mirada. That's where we went, and we saw him there with Bandit."

Caro's eyes grew round. "You went to the beach?"

"What's the matter with that? We rode the merry-go-round, and we ate lunch and talked with Tony, and we took the bus home. We didn't do anything wrong!"

Caro raised both eyebrows. "Don't yell at me. I never said you did." She waited a minute. "What's it like at the beach?"

Angie looked at her little sister. She thought of Caro staying in the apartment waiting for their mother to wake up. She thought of her walking on Bundy Street, eating by herself at the card table, playing solitaire behind a locked door. Then she thought of the green sea and the air that smelled of salt and the clouds that moved with the wind.

Feeling guilty about Con was bad enough. She couldn't handle this. "I'll take you there," she said, "and you can see for yourself."

She knew what Caro was thinking. Angie was making one of those "someday" promises that didn't mean a thing. But Angie did mean it.

"Come on." Angie grabbed her by the hand. "Right now we've got to go to Tony's."

They didn't have to wait outside the Deli for long. Tony was climbing off the bus at the corner. It took him a few minutes because of the hurdy-gurdy and because Bandit was sitting on his shoulder.

As soon as he recognized them, he smiled. "What a nice surprise. Two beautiful ladies waiting for me. Hey, Angie. What's the matter?"

"Oh, Tony, you've got to come quick. Con's hurt. I know he is. He's upstairs, and Bernice won't let me in." She took a breath. "Orly did it, Tony."

When Angie thought about it afterwards, she couldn't believe Tony had moved that fast. He scooted them back across the street, monkey and all, and stood impatiently while Angie unlocked her door.

"Now, both of you, wait here for me. Take care of Bandit. I'll be back in a little while."

"Wait!" Angie caught him by the arm. "Tony," she whispered, "will you ask Bernice why it's my fault?"

"Your fault?"

She nodded, unable to say any more. He put his hand on her head. "Leave it to Tony," he said.

Angie held her head in her hands and shut her eyes. Why was Tony taking such a long time? Could it be because—the thought made her so sick she felt dizzy—Con was ... dead?

Angie squeezed her eyes tighter. Her mouth was dry, and she couldn't swallow. She really was going crazy. Listen to that pounding in her head. *Thump! Thump! Thump!* No ... it was the door. Bandit made a terrible racket and began jumping up and down. That meant Tony was back.

For a second she couldn't get out of the chair. She

looked across the table just in time to see Caro scatter a deck of cards across the table and onto the floor. Caro started to pick the cards up, then stopped. Her lower lip was trembling.

Angie looked at her sister in surprise. Caro wasn't calm at all. That card game of hers was just a front to hide the way she really felt. Angie pushed back her chair and stood up. She was the oldest here, and it was about time to start acting like it. She went to the door and let Tony in.

"Hush!" he said to Bandit; then he went and sat on the arm of the sofa. Last time Tony was here, he'd found out that the arm was the safest place to sit. Both the two big cushions had broken springs.

Finally Tony turned to her. "Listen, Angie. Con's not all right, but he's going to be all right. Bernice told you the truth about that.

"Bernice is acting a little crazy," he went on. "She wanted to blame someone besides herself, so she picked on you. But it's not your fault, Angie. Not yours, and not Con's."

"Orly?" she asked, once the meaning of Tony's words had registered deep within her mind.

"He's gone. If we're lucky, he won't come back. He wanted Con to turn all the money he made over to him. That's what started all the trouble. He found out that Con had been saving a little bit."

Angie sat up and shook her head. "That's not fair. Con works hard, and Orly doesn't work at all."

"I didn't say it was fair. I said it's the way Orly wants it."

Angie swallowed. Her throat was dry. "Tony, what are we going to do?"

"We're going to eat a late dinner, and then you and Caro are going to bed. Don't expect to see Con for a few days, and don't go upstairs. He'll come down when he feels like it."

Tony got up and headed for the kitchen. "Let's just

hope that Orly's gone for good. That will solve a lot of problems."

He opened a can of soup and a box of crackers. "You mix up some powdered milk," he told Angie.

He heated the soup and poured it into three bowls. Angie wasn't hungry. She didn't intend to eat a thing, but Tony sat there until she did.

Then he stacked the dishes in the sink. "I'm taking Bandit home now," he said. "I want you girls to get some sleep. You did the right thing when you called me." He nodded his head in approval. "I'll check on Con in the morning. Leave it to me."

He closed the door softly behind him, and Angie turned the key in the lock. When she turned around, Caro was pulling the bed out from the wall and would have climbed in it with her clothes on if Angie hadn't stopped her.

Caro gave her a funny look. "You make it sound like my whole future depends on whether or not I sleep in my clothes."

Angie climbed into the bed beside her. "I don't know, Caro," she sighed. "Maybe it does."

In a few moments, Caro's breathing was steady and heavy. But Angie didn't go to sleep. She was thinking about what Orly had said. *I'll get you. One of these days when you're not looking, I'll find a way to get you.*

Angie stared at the shadowy ceiling with the plaster cracks that showed even in the dark. She sighed and turned her face to the wall. There was only one answer. She couldn't see Con anymore. The words kept repeating over and over in her head, like a cracked record. Con and she would live in the same apartment building, but they wouldn't be friends. Orly would hurt them both if he saw them together. Especially Con.

Angie used the end of her pillowcase to wipe away the tears. Without Con her life would be just like Caro's card game. She'd play it all alone.

5
A MOONLESS NIGHT

It was late on Wednesday afternoon when Orly returned. Angie was at Second Chance, the second-hand dress store she sometimes worked at, when she looked out the window and saw him coming down the street. A cold shiver started at the back of her neck and made her shudder.

"What's the matter with you?" Flo demanded. She owned the shop and the Original Maria's, the restaurant next door.

When Angie didn't answer, Flo came over to see what she was looking at.

"I was afraid of that," Flo sighed. "Poor Con. Now it's going to be the same old story over and over again. Orly won't let the boy out of his sight. He'll work him to the bone, but he won't lift a finger himself. And that temper!"

"Do you have anything more for me to do?" Angie asked Flo.

"Not this afternoon. But you can come back in the morning and help in the restaurant. I have to admit it, Angie, I'm always glad when school is out and I don't have to do all the work myself.... Say, Angie. Have you seen Con since ...?"

Angie shook her head. She hadn't seen him at all.

She'd been kind of hoping that today ... or tomorrow ... Oh, what was the use of hoping? Orly was back.

She went out on the sidewalk and up the steps of their apartment house next door. But she hesitated before she went inside. She was scared of Orly—and she wasn't ashamed to admit it.

"Hey, Angie. Wait up. I gotta talk to you."

For the first time in her life, Angie was glad to see Arnold Tooker. She watched while he stumbled on the bottom step and almost fell.

"Hey, man. There must be a loose board there."

There wasn't, but Angie let it go. She nodded toward the screen. "You might as well come in."

She followed him inside and glanced quickly around the hallway. No sign of Orly.

"Well?" she asked. "What do you want?"

Took began to whisper. "Unlock your door, for pete's sake. We can't talk out here."

Angie unlocked the door, but she didn't like this one bit. "Hurry up," she snapped. "I've got a lot to do."

"Go ahead and do it. I can wait." Took pushed past her and settled himself on the broken springs of the sofa.

Angie sighed. Now that he was in, she wasn't going to get rid of him until she heard what he had to say.

"OK, OK. Just make it quick, will you?"

"It's like this, Angie. I've got a great idea."

Angie groaned loudly.

"Now wait a minute. It really is a good idea. I know how to save Con."

Angie stared at his face. She knew now why Took always reminded her of a weasel. It wasn't so much the way he looked. It was the slyness at the back of his eyes.

"You know how to save Con? That's a laugh, Arnold Tooker. Since when did you ever think of anybody but yourself?"

He didn't answer. He just leaned his head against the

wall and waited.

Angie folded her arms and stood in front of him. "Go ahead and tell me," she said. "But make it quick."

Took raised his chin. When he stretched his neck like that, he looked like a skinny fish. "I'm gonna take him away from here. I've got a good place for him to go."

"Where?"

"To my uncle's place. He lives in Arizona. On a ranch. He needs extra hands." Took paused for effect. "That means he needs extra helpers."

Angie knew what it meant. She stared at him. "Are you telling the truth? Because if you're lying to me—"

"Honest! Why would I lie? Would I be dumb enough to go all the way to Arizona without a place to stay once I got there?"

Angie had to think about it. He was pretty dumb, but even Took couldn't be that stupid.

"Wait a minute. It costs money to go to Arizona."

"Me and Con will jump a train. Nothin' to it. I've done it before, just for kicks. And we'll leave at night. That way, nobody will miss us for a while."

Nobody will miss you at all, Angie thought.

"And then ..." Took puffed himself up as if he had just won a prize. "... then it'll be too late. They'll never find us."

"What's the matter with you? Of course they'll find you. All they have to do is look for you at your uncle's!"

Took blinked rapidly. He did a lot of that when he was nervous. "Yeah. Well, you'll be the only one who knows where we are. I'll ... uh ... give you the address."

Angie looked at Took and narrowed her eyes. She looked at him like that until he began twisting his belt flap. How much was the truth? With Took, it was hard to tell. He acted like a liar all the time. But if any of this was true, it might be a chance for Con to get away from Orly and Bundy Street. His only chance.

"Listen, Took. Why are you telling all this to me?"

"You're his girl, ain't ya? C'mon, Angie. Admit it. You'll be the first one to see him when he comes downstairs. You tell him, Angie. He always listens to you."

Angie didn't answer. She kept on staring until he began to blink and had to look at the floor.

"OK! OK! I already told Con about goin' to Arizona—a couple a weeks ago—but he wasn't interested. He said he was goin' to get a scholarship or somethin'. He's crazy, ya know. There's only one way to get out of Bundy Street, and that's to run."

Took was like a piece of cellophane paper, Angie thought. She could see right through him. "Do you have to run from something, Took? Why are you so anxious to get away?"

His face turned red, but he answered her smoothly, as if he had been practicing. "Bundy Street is boring. I'm sick of it. I need a change."

Took got up and went to the door. "Con better come with me, Angie. You can tell him. You're the only one he ever listens to." He stuck his chin out defiantly. "Anyway, if you think I'm gonna go up and knock on Orly's door, you're off your rocker!" He paused, his hand on the knob. "Ya just gotta decide whether ya want Con safe in Arizona or dead in Los Angeles. Think about it, Angie."

Her heart skipped a beat, leaving her with the feeling that someone had just punched her.

Took opened the door to go, but he didn't leave, because Con was standing on the other side, his hand raised, about to knock. Nobody moved.

Slowly Con lowered his arm. It was black and blue from his wrist to the hem of his short-sleeved T-shirt. His jaw was swollen, and the skin around both eyes was purple. The bridge of his nose stuck out like a golf ball was caught under the skin. When he started to talk, he looked as if it hurt him to open his mouth.

"What are you doing here?" he asked Took.

"I came by to ... uh ... Con, your face is a mess!"

Angie didn't say anything at all. She just stood there and stared at Con. He was standing on his own two feet, and he could talk, but that was about all. He tried to smile at her.

"Oh, Con!" Her voice choked, and she turned away.

In a second, Con was beside her. "Don't, Angie. Come on. Please don't do that." He put his bruised arms awkwardly around her shoulders.

"I'm sorry," she sobbed. "You don't know how sorry I am."

"Hey! You sound like you did it. What's the matter with you?"

"It wouldn't have happened if you hadn't been with me that afternoon."

"Angie, it would have happened if I'd been home. Our being at La Mirada just gave him an excuse."

An excuse. That's all Orly needed to hurt Con all over again. She couldn't let that happen. Angie glanced quickly toward the door. If Orly knew they were together right now ... She felt all mixed-up inside. Part of her was so glad to see Con that nothing else mattered. The other part kept remembering what Took had said: *Ya gotta decide whether ya want Con safe in Arizona or dead in Los Angeles. Think about it, Angie.*

"Listen, Con," she began. Then she had to stop a minute. She knew what she had to say. But it was so hard to make the words come out.

"Listen, Con. We ... can't see each other anymore."

Con looked at her a minute, as if he didn't quite understand what she had said. Then his face softened, and he put his hand on her arm "You're scared, Angie, and I don't blame you. But this isn't the way. Look, I'll get a job like Orly wants me to. That'll keep him happy for a while. No ... Angie, don't look at me like that. I'm not quitting on you. I'll go back to school someday. Right now I have to figure out how to live with Orly until I can figure out a way to get us both out of here."

Took gave a loud laugh. "You won't last that long, buddy. I mean ... look at yourself, man. You're gonna get killed hangin' around here."

"That's the chance I have to take." Con tried to smile. It made him look worse than ever.

Took was beginning to sound angry. "Why?" he demanded. "Tell me why you wanta hang around here?"

Con looked at Angie. "I've got my reasons," he said.

Angie closed her eyes. "Oh, Con," she whispered. "Those reasons aren't good ones anymore. Orly means what he said. We can't see each other again."

"Cut it out, Angie. There's no point talking like that."

"I'm serious, Con. Orly wants you to stay away from me, and that's what you're going to do. I can't stand seeing you like this. Don't you know that the next time could be worse?" Angie took a deep breath. "Look, I don't trust Took either, but this is a chance for you to get away from here. It may not be the best deal in the world, but it might be the only way. ..."

"Angie ... wait. Listen."

"No, Con. You listen." There was only one thing she could say now that might change his mind, and it made her feel like a coward to say it.

"If you decide to stay, Con, we're ... both going to be losers."

Took stood up. "Hey, that's right, man. Angie might have her turn. How would ya like to see her lookin' like you look now? Boy, there won't be much left of her when Orly throws *her* against a wall."

Con stared at Took. It was as if he had just realized what Orly's threat really meant. He reached out for Angie with one arm and buried his bruised face in her hair.

When he raised his head, his eyes looked as if he had just opened them after a bad dream—and discovered that things were even worse when he was awake.

41

"Then there's nothing left for me to do but leave," he said. But he kept holding on to Angie with one arm, as if he never intended to let her go.

"What's the matter? Scared to take a chance?" Took asked, knowing Con needed one final push.

"Take a chance! Don't you think I take a chance just by living in the same house with Orly? I'm afraid all right, but not afraid of taking a chance."

Angie lifted her face close to his. "Then take a chance on staying alive ... for both of us," she said.

He looked at her for a long minute. Then he put out his free hand and cupped it around the side of her face. Finally, he let both arms drop so that he wasn't touching her anymore. His voice was low and steady when he spoke to Took.

"Were you going to hitch a ride, or what?"

Took gulped, like a fish out of water, then found his voice. "Nah. That's too dangerous. I'm gonna hop a train. It's safe, and it's free."

"When do you want to leave?"

Took's eyes lit up. "Why not tonight? Nothin's keepin' me here."

Con was already organizing. "Listen, Took, you wait here while I get some things from upstairs." He hesitated. "Have you got an extra jacket? Orly has mine."

"You can have my poncho," Angie said quickly. It was warm, and she wanted him to have it. She went to the closet and pulled it out. She folded it carefully and handed it to Con.

As soon as the door slammed behind Con, Took began to talk. "Boy, Angie, I'll have to hand it to you. You really knew how to convince him. I owe ya one for that, Angie. I really owe ya one."

"Oh, shut up, Took. *Please* shut up!"

In a few moments she heard Con's footsteps. The door opened, and he stood there. He was carrying her poncho, and he had a canvas bag slung over one shoulder.

"Have you got your things?" he asked Took.

Took snorted. "Man, everything I got is on my back."

"Then let's get moving."

Took threw his arm around Con's shoulder. "Right, buddy. You just stick with Took, and everything's goin' to be OK." He gave Angie a wink.

She ignored him and looked at Con, still standing in the doorway.

It wasn't too late. She still had time to reach out her hand and pull him into the room. She could tell him she didn't really want him to go. She could keep him here ... on Bundy Street.

But she didn't move.

"Thanks for the poncho," he said. His eyes held hers for a long second. When he spoke, his voice was shaking. "I'll be back for you, Angie," he told her. "Someday, I'll be back." Then he stepped backwards into the hallway and pulled the door closed behind him.

She went to the kitchen window and watched as they crossed the street. Con walked tall, she thought. He held his head up, and he walked tall.

Only after she couldn't see him any longer did she begin to cry. She stood in a corner of the kitchen and put her face to the wall. Finally she sank down in a heap on the linoleum.

She didn't know how long she stayed there, but when Caro came over and put her hand on her shoulder, she was sure that her sister knew what had happened. Caro must have been in the kitchen the whole time, standing in the dark listening.

Because she leaned over and said, "It's dark outside, Angie. It's awfully dark. There isn't even a moon."

6
A HOLE IN THE DARKNESS

Angie wasn't asleep. She lay on the bed and stared into the darkness. It was thick and black. She couldn't find any holes in it at all.

Her mother had come home quite a while ago. That meant it was pretty late.

Where was Con now? What was he doing? She tried to imagine him sitting on the floor of a boxcar. After a train left Los Angeles, it wasn't long before it reached the town of Indio and open desert. That's probably where Con was now. On the desert.

Would Con ever realize that she'd wanted him to go for his own good? Not just because she was afraid of Orly. It didn't matter, she told herself, as long as he was safe. She thought of the way his bruised face had looked. At least Orly would never do that to him again.

"Angie!"

The sound was like a scratch at the door.

"Angie!"

There it was again. Louder. Urgent.

She sat up in bed. Who in the world would be out in the hallway at this time of night?

Angie felt her way across the dark room and opened the door as quietly as she could. The night-light in the hallway was bright, and she blinked for a few seconds; then she focused on the figure in front of her.

Took!

Arnold Tooker was standing there staring back at her with eyes that bulged alarmingly. His face was streaked with dirt, and his T-shirt was torn. One leg of his jeans was hanging open in a loose flap like someone had sliced it with a knife. His skinny chest was going up and down, and his open mouth made a strange, whistling sound every time he took a breath.

He was trying hard to say something. "Your ... your ..." Then he began to cough.

Angie pushed past him and looked into the hall. Then she went to the front door and looked outside. Something inside her turned upside down.

"Took!" Her voice was loud as she whirled to face him. "Where's Con?"

Her back was against the apartment house door now, blocking the way. Took stood, half crouching, in front of her. His eyes moved rapidly, like a small animal's. "Your fault ..." he whispered. "All your fault ..."

Then she saw the poncho. It had been wadded up under Took's arm. He pulled it out—what was left of it—and threw it at her feet. It looked like someone had put it through a meat grinder. She bent to pick it up and saw the stains—felt the sticky wetness that was already drying—stiffening the fabric as if it had been splattered with a dark red starch.

Took was still trying to get his breath, but his voice came out louder now. "Not ... my fault," he gasped. "Con ... he wouldn't listen."

Behind him, Angie saw Caro's face in the doorway. Then a light went on in the apartment.

"I knew what to do.... I told him. ... But he ..." Took's voice rose; then he seemed to choke on his words. He bent over, coughing hard.

Angie grabbed him by the arm and shook him. When he kept on coughing, she shook him again. "Tell

45

me!" she yelled. "What did Con do? What happened to him?"

Angie saw her mother. "Angie ..." she said. "What in the world?"

Took whirled to look at her. Then he began edging toward the door.

"Oh, no, you don't!" Angie stood firmly against the screen, blocking his way. "You're not going anywhere, Arnold Tooker, until you tell us about Con. Where is he? And why aren't you with him?"

"I tried to help him. Ya gotta believe me, Angie. I told him ... told him to wait ... to get on a train that ... wasn't moving. He was in a hurry. That was your fault, Angie. 'Don't be a fool, Con!' That's what I told him. But he ... jumped anyway."

Took shuddered. He bent over and held his stomach as if he hurt inside. "I can't stand it," he moaned. "I don't wanta remember."

Angie's mother came over quickly and put her hands on his shoulders. "Listen to me, Took! You have to tell us as fast as you can. What happened to Con, and where is he right now?" She didn't look sleepy anymore, and her voice had a command to it that surprised Angie. Her mother was taking control, just like Tony Genovese would.

Took pointed at Angie. "It was her fault. She gave him the poncho. It was the poncho that caught on the wheels. Con jumped.... But it caught and ... pulled him ... Ohhhh!" Took moaned.

"Pulled him where? Took! Listen to me! What happened to Con?" Angie's mother gave him a shake. "Tell me. Right now!"

Took looked at her. "It pulled him under. That's what I've been tellin' ya. We were in the train yards. That poncho of Angie's caught, and it ... pulled him under ... the wheels. Then ... I came straight here for help."

Took was crying again, but he wasn't making any

noise. His face was all screwed up, and his shoulders shook, but no sounds came out.

"Have you told anybody else?" Angie's mother asked.

Took shook his head. She let go of him and ran past Caro into the apartment. In a few seconds, Angie heard her voice.

"Operator ... yes ... this is an emergency!"

Angie looked down at the ragged poncho. She wanted to push open the screen and run outside. All the way to the train yards. She wanted to find Con. But her legs wouldn't move.

The apartment house door was supposed to be closed at night. No one could get into the hallway without a key. But Took had gotten in. There was only one key he could have used. Con's. And Con always carried it on his belt.

She looked at Took. "How did you get in?" she demanded.

"With Con's key," he told her. "I had to use it. How else was I gonna open the door?"

"You're telling me you took time to unhook Con's key from his belt? Then you took time to take off his poncho? And then you took time to come all the way back here?" Her voice was shaking, but she made herself go on. "Took, you don't have any brains at all. You should have called for help!"

Her mother was back now, shaking her head at Angie to stop. "I've just called the police, and the paramedics, too. It isn't very far from here to the train yards, Angie. I'm sure Took didn't waste any time."

Took stretched up his neck. He'd stopped crying, but his face was all red, and he was sniffing loudly. "Yeah. That's right. I came real fast. And ... listen, Angie. I didn't waste much time, because he wasn't wearin' the poncho anymore. I picked it up off the ground."

Angie looked at him suspiciously. "And then you left

47

him? Just like that?"

"He ... didn't care. He didn't know if I was there or not." Took started holding his stomach again. "Con ... he was makin' a lot of noise. Yellin' and screamin', and ... I just had to get out of there."

Took sat down abruptly on the hall floor and shut his eyes. "At first, Angie ... listen ... ya gotta believe me. I tried to help. But I didn't know what to do."

He squeezed his eyes shut tighter. "I never saw anybody before with ... his legs almost gone ..."

"Oh!" Angie's mother clapped both hands over her mouth. When she took them away, they were pressed tightly together in front of her. "Took, look at me. Do you know what you're saying?"

Took didn't open his eyes. But his head nodded. "The train got his legs. They were ... run right over."

Angie's mother turned and started up the stairs. "I have to tell Bernice," she said. "I don't want any of you to move."

Angie didn't move. She held her poncho and looked at Took sitting on the floor. She didn't let herself think about what he'd just said. Took was a liar. He'd always been a liar. There wasn't any point in listening.

She could hear her mother talking to Bernice upstairs. A door slammed. Then Orly's voice joined the other two. "If the kid ran away," he said, "he can stay away. You tell him that. He knows what's waiting for him if he tries to come back here."

"You don't understand what's happened." It was Angie's mother talking. "I'm trying to tell you that there's been an accident."

"Listen," Bernice interrupted. "Con has always been able to take care of himself. If he wants to stay out all night, that's his problem."

"Will you listen! The boy's been hurt!"

"Says who?" Orly asked loudly.

"You really don't care, do you?"

48

"Sure I care. I care about getting some sleep."

The door slammed. Then the only sounds in the building were Angie's mother's footsteps, running across the landing and down the stairs.

Con runs down the stairs every morning. He has good legs. He can run anywhere. Angie narrowed her eyes at Took. He was a dirty liar. She wasn't going to believe him. She wasn't!

From somewhere at the edge of her mind a sound began. It hung on the air, rising and falling like something lost in the night.

That's the way sirens always sound, Angie thought. Lonely and far away. But these sirens weren't far away. They were getting louder.

She saw Took get up off the floor and go to the screen door. Then she saw her mother push right past him. She was wearing jeans and a blue shirt.

She turned once in the doorway and looked at Angie. "Somebody needs to go and be with Con. No, Angie," as Angie moved forward. "I think you had better stay here. All three of you should stay right where you are. I'll get Tony to come with me, and I'll telephone as soon as I find out ... anything."

She turned and ran down the steps. Red lights throbbed around her. For a few seconds, Bundy Street looked like it was on fire. Then two police cars and an ambulance screamed down the block and squealed their tires as they turned hard.

"They're heading for the train yards," Took said.

His voice was a dull knife, cutting painfully into Angie's consciousness. She felt Caro close beside her. She felt Caro's hand in hers.

Took pushed the screen door open and went outside. He stood for a few minutes at the top of the steps; then he slowly walked away into the darkness.

After a minute, she opened the door and went outside herself, pulling Caro by the hand. They stood there on the porch, leaning close together. Finally, the sirens began their steady wailing. They were coming from the train yards this time.

Angie followed the sounds in her mind. Along Sixty-fourth ... coming closer now. She closed her eyes tightly as the ambulance screamed along Bundy Street. When she opened them, the red lights had disappeared, and she saw, instead, the yellow neon lights of the Universal Mission.

PRAYER CHANGES THINGS.

The words blinked at her out of the darkness like a giant advertisement. She stared hard. Angie had always had serious doubts about that sign. Oh, it wasn't because she didn't believe in God. Everybody on Bundy Street believed in God, and they said his name all the time just to prove it. But she and Con had talked about it, and they had decided that God had better places to spend his time.

Caro began pulling at her hand. "I'm real cold, Angie. Can we wait inside?"

Angie looked down at her sister. "You go on in. I'll be right there."

Angie stared at the sign a few more minutes. It looked like someone had cut yellow stencils out of the sky and made little holes in the darkness.

When she went inside, Caro was lying in the bed with covers pulled up over her nose. Her eyes were shut, but Angie knew she wasn't asleep.

Angie shook her head slowly back and forth. Things hadn't turned out the way she had planned them at all. Instead of safe in Arizona, Con was ... She squeezed her eyes shut, but she could still see him in her mind. He was probably in the emergency room at West Side General Hospital.

Angie clenched her fists and felt the poncho with her fingers. She was still holding it, tight against her stomach. It was stiff now, where the blood had dried.

Con's blood.

"Let him live," she whispered. "Please. He hasn't done anything wrong. Please let him live.... Let him live. Let him live!"

The words came from somewhere so deep inside her that pretty soon she didn't have to say them.

She didn't know how long she sat at the card table. But she knew her arms ached and her mouth was dry. When the phone rang, she was surprised to see that the room was light. The night had passed, and it was morning.

7
WEST SIDE GENERAL

Angie picked up the receiver.

"Angie! Is that you?"

It was her mother's voice.

Angie swallowed and cleared her throat. "Hello," she whispered.

"Listen, Angie. I have good news. Con is alive. He's badly hurt, but he's alive."

Then she heard Tony's voice. It sounded far away, but she could make out the words.

"It's all right, Evelyn," he said softly. "That's enough for now. We'll tell her the rest later."

Then his voice was louder. "Angie? This is Tony. Listen, Angie. We'll be home in a few minutes."

Angie's voice cracked. "What are you going to tell me later?"

Tony took a quick breath. She could hear it, because he was talking so close to the phone. "Angie," he said finally, "I can't talk any longer. I'm going to bring your mother home right now, and I'll tell you everything when we get there. It's been a long night, Angie. How about making something hot for us to drink?"

"OK, Tony." She hung up the phone and stood looking at it a minute before she went into the kitchen.

Had her prayer changed things? Con was alive, and that's what she'd asked for, wasn't it? Then why did she have such a bad feeling inside of her?

She reached in the cupboard and took out a can of powdered chocolate drink, pried off the top, and measured some into a small pan. Then she added water, lit the fire, and began to stir.

She shivered, and went into the bedroom and pulled on jeans and a heavy sweater. She put gym socks on underneath her sneakers. But when she went back to the kitchen, she shivered again.

A taxi pulled up in front of the apartment. Angie went to the window and saw Tony get out; then he reached out his hand to help her mother. Taxis were expensive. She wondered why they hadn't walked. It was only a little over half a mile to the hospital.

Her mother looked up toward the window. Her face was white and the skin seemed stretched tight. She took hold of Tony's arm, and the two of them stood there. Tony looked at her mother; then they started slowly toward the house.

Angie went to the stove and turned off the fire. The front door opened and closed, and still she stayed in the kitchen.

Con is alive, she kept telling herself. *Con is alive.*

"Angie..." Her mother's voice was a whisper from the other room. Then she was in the doorway.

Angie didn't answer. She opened the cupboard and took down three cups. Then she carefully began to pour the hot chocolate. She put the cups on a tray.

When Angie turned around with the tray in her hands, her mother was right there, watching her. She had a fake everything's-all-right smile on her face.

"That looks good," she said.

She reached out and took the tray; then she stood back and waited for Angie to go in front of her. Angie didn't have much choice. She went into the living room and sat down at the card table with Tony. She didn't look at either of them.

Nobody said anything for a few minutes. Her mother passed around the chocolate, and they all pretended to taste it. When Tony cleared his throat, her mother jumped, the table wobbled, and the hot chocolate made a dark brown pool around each cup.

Angie went to the kitchen for a dishrag. She could hear them whispering in the other room.

When she came back, she saw Caro with the covers still pulled up around her nose and her eyes shut tight. Angie wished she could crawl back in bed and be ten years old again.

"You know, Angie," her mother began, "this whole thing has been terrible, but the important part to re- member is that Con is still alive." She shook her head. "It's a miracle. I don't know how they saved him."

Then, "The thing is, Angie, he was so badly hurt, that... there were complications. His ... his ..." Her mother said the rest so quickly that it sounded like one long breath. "Angie, Took told us the truth. Con's legs were caught under the train. They were taken almost off."

"So ... he's really going to be all right?" Angie asked. She looked at her mother, then at Tony.

It was Tony who finally answered her. He took both of her hands in his big ones and held them tightly. "Now listen to me," he said. "Con is going to live, but he's not all right. He's going to have to live without his legs."

Angie stared at him. "You said they were almost off! Almost isn't all the way. The doctors can sew them on. I know they can." Her voice was getting louder, shriller. "They have to. Con needs his legs!"

"The doctors did try, Angie. They tried all night. They finally had to amputate to save his life."

Amputate? Angie opened her mouth, but she couldn't say the word. They had cut off Con's legs.

"Oh, no! I don't believe you." She stood up quickly and shook her mother by the arm. "Go back and tell them to try again." She looked at Tony. "Please, Tony!"

"It's too late," he told her. "Angie, they saved his life. You have to be thankful for that."

She clenched both fists. "If they don't give Con his legs back, I'll never forgive them! Oh, Tony! Please go back and tell them!"

"I can't, Angie." Tony's voice was rough. "The legs are gone. You'd better accept that, or you're not going to be able to help Con at all."

"It was Orly's fault," she exclaimed. Her mother and Tony stopped talking and looked at her. "And ... Took's ... and this whole stupid street's!"

"Wait a minute," said her mother. "I'm not so sure about that. Con had his problems. But none of them made him run away until last night. No, Angie. I think something else happened to Con. He never would have run away ... unless he thought he had no other choice."

They were both looking at Angie, as if she knew what had happened.

Her mother put her arm around Angie. "We'd all like to find somebody to blame. But what good would it do? Instead, we'd better start thinking about what's going to happen when Con comes home."

Angie couldn't think about that. Suddenly, she had to get out of there. She pulled away from her mother and walked across the room.

"Angie, wait. Where are you going?"

She didn't know. She didn't care. "To the hospital," she lied.

"Angie, it's too soon. They won't let you see him."

Tony put his hand on her mother's arm. "They might," he said. "They just might."

Angie left. She didn't know if her mother called her again or not, because she didn't listen. She pushed open the front door and stood alone on the porch. But she didn't look at the neon sign across the street. She knew what it said, and she didn't believe it.

She looked, instead, at the stray weed that was still trying to grow up the side of the steps. "It won't do you any good," she said out loud. "If you stick your head up around here, you'll just get it chopped down."

She reached out one foot as if to smash it, then stopped. A tiny, heart-shaped leaf was straining upward, standing erect on its fragile stem. It was walking tall, she thought, just as Con had walked last night. Well, let it try. What was one more weed on Bundy Street?

Angie began walking. She didn't care which way she went; she just moved through the fog, letting it cover her like Caro's blanket. Maybe the fog would last all day, and she would never have to come out.

But it lifted, just the way it always did in June. One minute it was heavy and wet and thick, and a few seconds later it turned to wispy trails.

Angie stared across the street at the complex of buildings. They seemed to be growing larger and larger as the fog cleared. A red sign at the end of the drive said EMERGENCY in large square letters. There was no other identification, but Angie knew where she was. She and Con had walked past the back side of West Side General Hospital a hundred times.

Angie shuddered. She stood at the corner and pushed the traffic button on the side of the lamppost. She jammed both hands into the pockets of her jeans, and felt her right index finger curl around a loop of hard metal.

She pulled it out and stared at the shiny brass ring. She had forgotten all about it. Angie tried to remember how happy they had been that day, and how they had laughed as they walked together up the hill. But all she could think of was the look in Con's eyes when she had told him they couldn't see each other again.

Angie blinked her eyes hard. She couldn't see very well right now, but she knew where she was going. When the light changed, she quickly crossed the street.

8
ROOM 202

Angie stood at the counter for a long time, but nobody seemed to notice her. She cleared her throat. "Excuse me."

The woman raised her head. "Did you want something?" She looked at Angie, surprised.

"I wonder ... I mean ... could you tell me where ..." Angie stopped and tried again. "There was an accident last night at the train yards," she said.

The nurse's face changed. She suddenly looked like a human being. "I'm afraid you can't see that patient now. But you can go upstairs and see if the desk can tell you anything." She hesitated, and looked at Angie curiously. "Are you family?"

"I'm his sister," she lied.

The nurse gave her a sympathetic nod. "That must have been your mother and father who were here last night." It was a statement, not a question, and Angie let it go. The nurse was pointing to an open doorway.

"Look, honey, you just go through that door and on to the end of the hall. Turn left. The elevator is around the corner. Go upstairs to the first floor and look for information. Maybe they can tell you how your brother is this morning."

Angie thanked her and started down the long corridor. When she found the elevator, it was open and empty. She pushed the number-one button and went slowly up.

The lobby was very quiet. The telephone on the information desk rang. It had a muffled sound, and when a woman in a pink uniform answered it, she spoke so softly that Angie could hardly hear her voice.

She went to the desk and waited. The phone sank soundlessly into its cradle, and the pink lady looked up. "Can I help you?" she whispered.

It gave Angie the creeps. Why was it so quiet? Nobody was sick in here. To her horror, she hiccuped.

The woman's eyebrows went up. "Can I help you?" she repeated.

Angie needed to go somewhere and hold her breath and count to ten and drink a glass of water. Instead, she tried to look steadily at the raised eyebrows. "I'd like some information, please."

"The name?"

"Con...I mean, Howard. Howard Conway. He's...my brother. There was an accident last night. A train..." She had to stop and swallow. She hiccuped again.

This time the woman pretended not to notice. "Oh, yes. I know about that. I'm sorry."

"Could ... could you tell me how he is?" Angie closed her mouth quickly.

The woman picked up the phone and dialed a single number. "Information for Howard Conway," she said. "Yes, I'll wait." Angie held her breath and counted to ten.

The woman began talking into the phone. "I see. Yes, I understand." She smiled at Angie. "Your brother is doing as well as can be expected this morning. That's pretty good news, considering all he's been through."

"Can I see him?"

"I'm afraid not. It's too soon for visitors. Why don't you go home, dear, and come back tomorrow?"

"Could you tell me his room number ... so I won't

have to ask when I come back tomorrow?"

She consulted her chart. "Room 202," she said. "One floor up, at the end of the hall."

"Thank you very much." Angie turned and started toward the elevator.

"Just a minute, Miss Conway. That's the wrong way." The pink lady pointed firmly to the hospital entrance.

The next hiccup was loud—and painful. Angie silently blessed it. She waved her hand at the drinking fountain next to the elevator doors and held her throat. "I need a drink of water," she said. And hiccuped again.

Angie drank the water slowly. When she'd had all she could stand, she kept the faucet running and pretended to drink some more. The elevator door opened, and two nurses came out. Angie lifted her head and watched as they walked to the desk and stood directly in front of it.

Angie straightened up and stepped into the elevator. The doors slid shut; then she pushed two, and began to move.

The elevator stopped, and Angie got off. There was a small waiting room with a table, some magazines, and three chairs at that end of the hall. There was also a door that said Positively No Admittance. That made it easy. Angie turned right and started walking in the only possible direction.

Room 232 was first on her left. She could smell the flowers clear out in the hallway. She glanced in and saw them, displayed on the dresser.

222 … 220 … 218 … Angie checked the room numbers off one by one. She felt as if she were moving on a conveyor belt, and nothing could stop her until she reached the end of the line.

But something did stop her. It was a voice that came from the nurses' station halfway down the hall. "Just a minute! Where are you going?"

The voice belonged to a large, dark-haired woman

who wore a cap with two black bands and held a pencil as if she were carrying a weapon.

Angie pointed toward the end of the hall. "Room 202. I'm going to see my ... brother."

The nurse frowned and consulted her charts. "Not without special permission, you're not. The only one in that room young enough to be your brother would be 202A, and he just came back from surgery. You would have to be his mother to get in there this soon."

"She ... that is, our ... mother couldn't come," Angie said. "That's why I'm here." They didn't have to worry about Bernice, she thought.

"It must have been something pretty important to keep her away at a time like this," the nurse muttered. She shook her head firmly at Angie. "Rules are rules."

Angie looked desperately down the hall. She was so close. She felt like making a run for it. "Oh, please!" she begged. "It's so important. He won't have to talk or anything. I just need to see him. I want to tell him ..." Her voice broke, and she stopped. It wasn't any of their business what she wanted to tell him.

"What's going on here?"

Angie felt a hand on her shoulder and looked up at a tall, thin man. He was wearing something that looked like green pajamas and a flat, green cap.

"This girl was on her way to room 202, Dr. Stinson. She says she's the young man's sister."

Dr. Stinson patted Angie on the shoulder. "I'm sorry," he said. "Your brother needs all the rest he can get. We just brought him out of the intensive care unit, and it's really too soon for visitors. But come back tomorrow." He gave her another smile. "Why don't you leave your name with the nurse? We'll tell him you were here."

What was the use? She couldn't fight both of them. Angie blinked back the tears and said her name. "Angie. Just tell him Angie was here."

The expression on the doctor's face changed.

"You're Angie?" He took her by the arm and started down the hall, pulling her behind him. "It's all right," he said to the startled nurse. Then, to Angie, "He's been asking for you. Says your name over and over."

Now that she was almost there, Angie wasn't in such a hurry. She pulled back at the doorway. She wanted to stand there for a few seconds and look into the room, to see without being seen.

There were lights in the room, but around the first bed it was darkened, shaded and protected by a large screen and by a gray curtain that slid on rings attached to a metal rod suspended from the ceiling. Con must be behind the curtain.

Dr. Stinson stepped into the room and gently pulled the curtain back around the foot of the bed. Con's head was on a pillow. His eyes were closed, and his face was very white. The bruises that Orly had made stood out beneath his freckles like dark blots. His arms were resting on top of the light blanket. They had needles in them, strapped tight with adhesive and connected to long tubes, which were attached to bottles that hung upside down from a metal frame.

Angie made herself look at the rest of him. She sucked in her breath and looked away quickly. Where Con's legs should have been was a great, flat emptiness, covered by a blanket.

Con's head moved on the pillow. His eyes stayed shut, but he said her name. "Angie ..."

"I'm here, Con. It's me ... Angie." She didn't remember going through the doorway. She was only aware of standing close to the bed and watching his face.

His eyelids fluttered and opened. He frowned, trying to focus. "Angie?" He opened his hand, reaching his fingers toward the railing that stretched like a fence along the side of his bed.

She put one hand through the slats and touched him. He closed his fingers around hers. "I'm sorry, Angie.

I really messed things up."

She had to wait a minute before she could speak. She made herself breathe slowly. She took her free hand and wiped it across her eyes.

"It was my fault, Con. I told you to go. I was so afraid. I thought something … terrible would happen to you if you stayed."

He pressed her fingers. "Not your fault. I … know … what you were trying … to do."

He was so quiet, she thought he had gone to sleep. Just as she started to move her hand away, he opened his eyes and held on tight.

"Took?" he asked.

"He wasn't hurt."

Con nodded. "Good. I … tried to get him out of the way. He didn't see … the train until it was …" He closed his eyes and turned his head away.

Angie felt her jaw tighten. Took had lied. He hadn't tried to save Con at all. It was the other way around. If she didn't do anything else for the rest of her life, she was going to see that Took got what he deserved.

"My foot hurts, Angie. The right one. It's really bad. It's like I've got a cramp in it. Would you … rub it for me?"

She stared in horror at the bottom of the bed. Con didn't know! They hadn't told him!

He opened his eyes and looked at her. "What's the matter? Angie, what's wrong?"

The doctor's hand was on her arm. His voice was loud and too cheerful. "Visiting hours are over. Sorry, young lady. Time's up!"

He pulled her gently but firmly away from the side of the bed and stood like a large green shadow in her place. "Let's try to get a little rest," he said to Con. His right hand moved to a round red button at the head of the bed and pushed it twice. "I'll give you something for the pain," he promised.

Angie could see Con's fingers tightening around the

rails. He was trying to sit up. "What's the matter?" he cried. "I can't move my legs!"

A nurse rushed past Angie and pulled the gray curtain around the bed so that it was like a large tent with Angie on the outside.

"Con ..." she whispered. "Oh, Con!"

Then she backed out into the hallway and tried not to listen to the low, soothing voices that spoke to Con, telling him that everything was going to be all right.

"No ... no ..." he moaned. And then she didn't hear his voice at all.

She stood in the hall until the doctor came out. He put his arm around her. "He really thought his foot was hurting, Angie. It's something we call phantom pain. But don't worry. He's asleep now, and we'll keep him that way the rest of the day. Come back tomorrow. Come as often as you can. The boy is going to need all the family support he can get."

Angie nodded. But she didn't answer. She was hearing Con's voice asking, "What's wrong, Angie? What's the matter?" and the other voices—strangers' voices—telling him, "Never mind, son. Everything's going to be all right."

Lies! They were telling him lies. This whole thing started out as a giant, Took-type lie.

She looked up at the brass-plated numbers above the door. 202. The zero gleamed at her like an empty eye. Or a ring. A shiny, golden ring. That was a lie, too. A promise that never happened.

Angie turned and walked slowly down the hall. She took the elevator down to the first floor and pushed open one of the glass doors. The sun was shining outside. Horns were honking. Everything about the busy street was the same as it was every day. She felt like shaking her fist at God.

I don't know what you think you're doing, she wanted to say. *Why don't you make bad things happen to bad people?*

What do you want of me, anyway? she demanded. *Do you want me to believe that big sign over the mission? Well, I don't. I can pray all day for Con to get better, but I know that only tadpoles grow legs!*

Angie felt very tired. She didn't know what to do.

She dug down into her jeans for the brass ring. When the light wasn't shining on it, it was nothing but a dull piece of metal. That was how she felt. Dull. Like all the light had gone out of her.

She stopped at the first wire trash container on the sidewalk, and stood, turning the ring over and over in her fingers, trying to remember the way she and Con had felt that day at the beach. Quickly she dropped the ring into the trash. Angie hesitated. She shouldn't have done that. Maybe Con would have wanted her to keep it. She started to reach into the basket.

"Step back there! Watch out!"

Angie jumped out of the way as a truck from the sanitation department roared to a stop.

The man picked up the basket and dumped it quickly into the hungry scoop; then he held on to the side of the truck as it rolled away.

Angie took a deep breath and let it out slowly. She stood and stared into the empty trash basket. It looked just the way she felt. Empty.

"I don't know what to do," she whispered. "I need somebody to show me ..." She squeezed her eyes shut tight. "... to show me which way to go."

She waited. For a few seconds she wasn't even sure where she was. She only knew she had to stand there because she had lost her way, and she was waiting for directions.

She walked slowly. There wasn't any place for her to go now but back to Bundy Street. She knew the way there all by herself.

9
SECOND CHANCE

Orly was gone and Bernice with him. Tony said that most of the neighborhood had watched them leave. They had started coming downstairs in the morning, while Angie was still at the hospital. They had seemed to be in a big hurry, piling boxes on the sidewalk and leaving a trail of junk along the way. Nobody tried to stop them. Nobody asked them where they were going. Bernice stood alone, by the street, while Orly went and rented a broken-down truck. When they finally drove away, everybody stood out on the sidewalk and watched. But nobody said good-bye.

Took had disappeared, too. He hadn't been seen since last night.

It figured, Angie thought. It was just like Took to run away and hide. Last night she had wanted him to find a dark, creepy hole where he could starve to death and be eaten by rats. Today, she didn't care.

Now it was eleven o'clock in the morning, and she didn't know what to do. She couldn't go back to the hospital until tomorrow. And there wasn't anyone she could talk to here. Her mother had gone back to bed, exhausted. Tony had had to go across the street and open the Deli. All the other people on Bundy Street were talking about the accident. All but Caro. She was sitting alone in the apartment, playing solitaire.

Angie went up the stairs to apartment 2A. The door was open. She stood there a moment and looked in at the empty room where Con had lived. She couldn't get it out of her mind that Orly might still be here, behind a door, waiting in a closed closet. When she went in, she walked softly, as if someone were asleep.

Under the window was a pile of clothing. Orly and Bernice evidently didn't want to be bothered with Con's clothes any more than they wanted to be bothered with Con.

Angie wondered what they'd done with the rest of his things. She remembered the canvas bag that he had carried over one shoulder last night. No telling who had it now.

Suddenly Angie felt a little sick. She left the door of 2A standing open and went down the stairs.

She opened her own door and looked at Caro's startled face. She looked like somebody who had been caught sleepwalking. Solitaire wasn't a game with Caro anymore. It was the way she lived.

"Come on," Angie urged. "I need you to help me."

She went to the kitchen and came back with a pile of empty grocery sacks.

Caro put down her cards reluctantly. "Where are you going?"

"Upstairs."

Caro shook her head and picked up the cards. She carefully stacked them and began to shuffle. "I don't want to go up there."

Angie knew what Caro was thinking. It was safe in here. It was like crawling into bed and pulling the covers over your head. If you stayed there long enough, you might even forget about the things that happened outside.

Angie didn't blame Caro. But she wasn't going to let her get away with it.

"Listen, Caro. Con's apartment is empty. You don't

have to worry about Orly, because I was just up there, and he's really gone."

Caro shrugged and started shuffling the cards. Angie had never seen her like this before.

"Listen, Caro. I saw Con this morning." She swallowed and went on. "I got to talk to him. And he talked to me."

Caro put down her cards and watched Angie doubtfully. "When is he going to come home?"

"I don't know. That's why I want you to help me. We need to get his things out of the apartment. He can't go back there."

She knew Caro would understand what she meant. This whole side of Bundy Street was owned by a big company in Los Angeles. Whenever anybody missed a month's rent, a man in a black suit appeared at the door. Con's apartment wouldn't be empty long.

Caro nodded. She was beginning to look interested. She had that wise owl expression that she always wore when she was trying to figure something out.

"Well, come on then. This is all we need." Angie waved the grocery bags and opened the door. Caro was still sitting in the chair. "Look, Caro," she snapped, "you either want to help Con, or you don't!"

Angie went out in the hallway and started up the stairs. Before she was halfway up, she heard Caro behind her. Together they went through the rooms, looking for anything of Con's that might have been left behind. There wasn't much. Just the pile of clothes and his schoolbooks. He must have packed the rest in the missing canvas bag.

When they had finished, they closed the door of 2A and stood uncertainly in the hall.

"Where's Con going to live now?" Caro asked.

"I ... don't know." For the first time, Angie realized that Con didn't have a home.

"Could he live with us?"

Angie didn't know that, either. What would her

mother say? Mentally she rearranged the furniture to make room for Con. Would he be in a wheelchair? Probably. But he couldn't sleep in it. How would he get on the couch every night? How would he get up in the morning? How would he get dressed? Or take a bath?

"Let's worry about one thing at a time," she told Caro. "We have to find someplace to put these things where Orly will never find them."

They both thought of it at the same time. The room at the top of the house! Nobody went there unless they were on their way to the roof.

They hurried up the stairs and opened the door. There was the usual pile of boxes in one corner, but now they were stacked neatly, several feet away from the wall, leaving a large space behind.

Angie walked cautiously across the room and looked behind the boxes. No one was here now, but someone sure had been. A small candle stood upright on a chipped blue saucer. A can of bug spray stood against the wall. Two pillows were stacked neatly, one on top of the other. On top of the pillows was a dog-eared sports magazine. On the cover was a picture of a young man in a track suit with a number across his chest. The caption was KEEP RUNNING! Then she saw the sleeping bag.

Con had saved for a long time to buy that sleeping bag. She was with him when he had picked it out.

Caro recognized it, too. She put the sacks she was carrying against the wall. "I'll bet Con moved up here after that fight with Orly," she said. "It's perfect, Angie. He can live up here, and we can take care of him."

Angie smiled, but she didn't answer. She watched Caro as she busily took the clothes out of the sacks, folded them neatly, and separated them into piles. Angie didn't help her. And she didn't have the heart to tell Caro she was wrong. You had to have legs to climb to the top of the stairs.

"There!" Caro said, standing back to look at what she'd done. She glanced up at Angie expectantly. "Where are we going now?"

Angie stared at her in amazement. Was this the same Caro who had sat at the card table a little while ago? What had made her change?

Suddenly Angie remembered something Con had said once. *You have to have a plan. You can stand almost anything if you know you have a plan.* Well, Angie didn't have any plan at all. But she must have made Caro think she knew what she was doing. Caro was looking up at her now, waiting.

Before they reached the bottom of the stairs, Angie knew what they were going to do next.

Flo looked surprised when she saw them standing in the doorway of Second Chance. Flo did all the cooking next door at Maria's, and the clothes at Second Chance always smelled a little like hot tamales. The connecting door was open now, and Angie looked in. Lunch hour seemed to be over.

Flo always made it seem good to work at her place. "Thank goodness for you girls!" she exclaimed. "Caro, honey, would you water those plants against the wall? And Angie … that crowd drank all the coffee. How about getting another pot started?"

Caro did as she was told. She was bustling around, Angie thought, as if she owned the place. Angie measured the coffee carefully.

"It smells good," said Caro behind her. "It makes me think of bacon and eggs."

"Did you eat breakfast?" Angie demanded.

Caro shook her head.

"Neither did I!" Angie had forgotten that Flo had ears like a fox. She could hear right through walls.

She appeared suddenly in the doorway. "Lunchtime!" she announced.

Flo could make sandwiches faster than anyone

Angie knew. In a few minutes they all were sitting together at one of the clean tables. Angie looked skeptically at the tuna on wheat bread, potato chips, and a large, fat pickle.

Flo took a large bite, chewed, and swallowed; then she leaned one elbow on the table and wagged her finger in Angie's face.

"Did you see what I just did?"

Angie nodded.

"OK. Now you pick up your sandwich and do the same thing. I know exactly what you're thinking, Angie Rafferty, and I can tell you right now that you're not helping anybody if you starve yourself to death!"

OK, thought Angie. *But it will come right back up again.* She was surprised when it didn't. Her stomach gave a little lurch and accepted it.

"Well?" Flo said, leaning back in her chair.

Angie didn't say anything. She had tucked Con away in a corner of her mind, just the way she did when she got a bad grade in school. As long as she didn't talk about it, it didn't seem real—at least not until the report card came.

She felt Flo's hand on her arm. "Angie," Flo said gently. "What has happened, has happened. It's a fact. We have to talk about it."

There was no stopping Flo when she made her mind up to do something for your own good. "Listen to me," she ordered. "If you hide something bad away in your mind, it grows. Did you know that? It gets bigger and bigger until you feel like it's choking you. The only way you can cut it down to size is to tell somebody about it.

"It's like putting a period at the end of a sentence," Flo explained. "What you have to do right now, Angie Rafferty, is to put a period on yesterday. This is today— Thursday afternoon. Wednesday is over."

Angie thought she'd lived a hundred years since Wednesday. But it seemed like only a second ago that she'd walked down the hall of the hospital to Con's room. She said the only truth she could think of.

"It's so dark in Con's room."

Flo looked surprised. "Angie, have you been to the hospital?"

"It's so dark in there," she said again. "There aren't any flowers." Suddenly it seemed so unfair. "Other people have flowers, but Con only has the shades pulled down and the lights turned off ... and ... an old gray sheet pulled around his bed."

Flo looked at her a minute. Then she cleared her throat as if she'd found her voice all of a sudden. "Sometimes people can rest better in the dark, Angie. But you're right. We don't want Con to stay in the dark any longer than he has to."

She got up and fished around in a cupboard. In a minute she came back with a small bud vase made of pink and orange carnival glass.

"One flower is all it will hold," she said.

Caro sounded disappointed. "Only one?"

Flo set the vase in the middle of the table and put both hands on her hips. "What's the matter with one flower? Bouquets are nice, but they're so crowded you can only see the colors. Ask Old Lu. She's got a whole cart full of colors, and she knows that one single flower is best of all."

Caro wiggled in her chair. "What do you do when it dies?"

Flo sighed. "You go out and get a new one." She leaned over and looked at them hard. "Do you girls know what I'm talking about? One flower a day. One step at a time. Give Con something to look forward to, because he's not going to get better overnight."

Angie nodded slowly. Flo took all the confusion out of things. She made you think that you really knew what you were doing. It wouldn't be so hard going to the hospital tomorrow if she took a flower with her. She could tell Con about not getting confused, about only thinking of one day at a time. It was a little like having a plan. Angie had never had a plan of her own before.

Suddenly Flo clapped her hand to her head as if she'd just remembered something. "That boy, Angie! He was here early this morning."

That boy? An old, horrible feeling started to fill Angie, seeping through the pores of her skin like a bad taste. "You mean Took?"

Flo thought it over. "Well, I suppose it was Took. He was real jumpy and looked like he was about to be sick. He left something here, and said you would know what to do with it."

Flo went to the other room and came back with a canvas bag. It was Con's, and Angie could see by the bulges that it was still full.

Flo got up and began clearing the table. "If the two of you are through being useful around here, why don't you scoot out and have a look at Old Lu's flowers. I'll say this for them, they're fresher than Old Lu!"

Flo wasn't being unkind. She was trying to make Angie smile. Old Lu's flower cart was kind of a joke around the neighborhood. The blossoms really were pretty, and they were fresh, too. It was just that they didn't seem to go with Old Lu. She had worn the same clothes for as long as anyone could remember; her skin looked like the outside of a peach that had sat in the sun too long; and she always smelled like garlic, because she chewed it for whatever seemed to ail her.

Flo got up and went to the cash drawer at the back counter and took out a few bills. "Here's your pay for this morning." She looked at Caro, as if measuring her up and down. Finally, she nodded "You're a good worker, too," she said. "You can come back every day with Angie, if you want to."

Angie stared at Flo. Every day! She had never come every day before. Only when she had needed some money.

Flo must have read her mind, for she looked at Angie and nodded her head vigorously up and down. "That's what I said. Every day. You girls are growing up. If you want a job, you have to be dependable, and that means every day. Ten o'clock. That way you can watch Second Chance while I handle the kitchen. Then you can help me clean up after lunch. That leaves afternoons free for hospital visits. Well, what do you think?"

"Thanks, Flo. Thanks a lot."

Flo didn't answer. She began fishing around in her pocket for a handkerchief. She blew her nose hard; then she wiped the corners of her eyes.

"Smog," she said. "It's really bad today."

"Yeah," said Angie. "I know." She picked up Con's canvas bag. "See you tomorrow."

The girls walked past Second Chance on their way to Old Lu's cart. "I think I'm going to like working in there best of all," said Caro.

Angie nodded, but she didn't answer. She was thinking of all the things Flo had said: about putting a period on yesterday, and living one step at a time, and being dependable. It almost made her think that there might really be a second chance.

She felt the canvas bag over her shoulder and thought briefly of Took. He had disappeared again, and nobody cared enough to look for him.

She didn't care, either. She hoped he stayed away. Took didn't deserve a second chance.

10
THE WHEELS THAT TURN

The next afternoon, Angie bought a fresh flower to put in the vase that Flo had loaned her. She was walking along Bundy Street, on her way to the hospital, when she saw Chico.

"Hi, kid!" he said. Chico called everybody kid. "That was ... uh ... tough luck about the boy. Always liked him. Glad his old man's gone."

Angie nodded. "Me, too."

"You goin' to see him?"

She nodded again. "I'm on my way."

"Well, listen. Tell him ... to hang in there—and that Chico's thinkin' about him."

"I'll tell him."

When she reached his doorway and looked into the room, her knees turned to jelly. She couldn't think of anything but the emptiness at the bottom of the bed. Con was lying there, flat on his back. His eyes were wide open, staring at the ceiling. He didn't move at all.

Don't let him be dead. Please don't let him be dead, Angie pleaded silently as she set the flower vase on the nightstand by his bed. Then she reached out and touched the railing that separated her from Con. Her palms were wet and sticky against the cold metal.

"I bought you a flower, and Flo sent this vase," she said.

Con blinked. He closed his eyes and opened them. Then he looked up at the ceiling.

"Oh, Con," she breathed. "You're all right. I'm so glad you're all right!"

He turned his head slowly and looked at her. "Sure," he said. "I'm just fine. Couldn't be better!"

"Con … I—I'm sorry. You know I didn't mean it like that. Con, please look at me."

How could she have let herself say such a dumb thing? She took his hand in both of hers and rubbed his skin gently with the side of her thumb. Finally, she began to talk. First, she told him about what Chico had said. Then she told him about working at Flo's and about taking each day one at a time. She told him almost everything she could think of, and still he didn't answer her. There was only one thing she had left out.

"Orly's gone, Con. Tony doesn't think he'll be back."

That was when he turned his head towards her. "What about my mother?" he asked quickly.

Angie swallowed. She had forgotten about Bernice. "She … went with him, Con. Listen, I'm sure she's worried about you. You know how Orly is. She probably didn't have any choice."

Con shook his head. "She had a choice." He closed his eyes.

She stayed a while longer, just watching him breathe—in and out, in and out. Tomorrow would be better, she told herself.

But tomorrow was worse. Angie could hear Con's voice the second she stepped off the elevator. "Stay away from me!" he shouted. "I don't need any help from you people. I'm not going to that therapy place. What difference does it make if my muscles contract or not? I'm not going to be using them."

Angie ran down the hall and stood, gasping for breath, in the doorway. An orderly and two nurses were standing around Con's bed.

"C'mon, Con." The orderly's voice was gentle. "You'll really be glad you let us help you. Therapy isn't what you think it is. It's a great place. And it's really important that you start today. C'mon and give it a try."

But none of them moved to touch him. Con looked like he was ready to take on the first one who put out a hand.

A folding wheelchair was open and ready by the side of Con's bed. Angie saw it. It was like a whole world opening up inside her head. If they could just get Con into that chair, he would be on the move again.

"Con," she said gently, "if you were in the wheelchair, I could push you wherever you wanted to go."

One of the nurses looked at her gratefully and moved over so she could come closer to the bed.

"Big deal!" Con sneered. "I don't want to go anywhere. I just want to be left alone. By everybody!" He glared at them all. But when he looked at Angie, his eyes said: especially by you!

"You always were bullheaded," she told him. "But now you're worse. You're just plain stupid."

Con glared at her again. "Look who's talking! Nobody with any brains would want to come to a hospital to visit a freak." He took a breath. "Now why don't you get out of here and quit bothering me!"

"All right, Con. I'm going. But that doesn't change what I said." Angie was surprised to hear the sound of her own voice. It was low and steady and calm. "You are acting stupid, and ... you're being mean besides." Her voice dropped to an almost whisper. "You know why I came to see you. You know I'll do anything in the world ..." She took a deep breath. "But if you don't want to see me ... I guess I won't be back."

She didn't remember going through the doorway and turning down the hall. All the way to the elevator, she kept thinking about the way Con had looked when she'd said those last words. He didn't seem like Con at all.

She hesitated a second; then she pushed the button. The door clanked open, and she was already inside when someone called, "Wait a minute!"

Angie pushed the open button and waited. One of the nurses from Con's room appeared.

"He wants you," she said.

Angie nodded and moved out of the elevator to follow her all the way back to Con's room.

The other nurse and the orderly seemed to be gone, but Dr. Stinson was waiting just inside Con's door. He came out into the hallway and put one hand on Angie's shoulder.

"Go on in, Angie," he said gently. 'You can stay as long as you want."

He paused. "Angie, it's so important for Con to let us help him. It's vital for him to start therapy as soon as possible. Maybe you can talk to him."

He gave her a little shove and shut the door quietly behind her. She didn't say a word to Con, just walked over close to the bed. From where she stood, she could see the wheelchair.

Con was staring at the sheets that covered the bottom of his bed. Angie thought she knew what he was thinking. But she didn't speak, and she didn't reach out to touch him. That awful word that Con had said kept rolling around in her mind, blocking out everything else.

Freak, freak, freak.

She was furious with Con for calling himself that. Legs or no legs, she was going to make him apologize. Not to her, but to himself.

Finally he cleared his throat. "Listen, Angie ..."

She didn't look at him. "I'm listening."

"Angie, I'm sorry. It's been a rotten day. I've been feeling ... bad inside. And then they (he waved his hand toward the door) had to come in here and start

77

telling me what to do. Look, Angie, I'd never be mean to you. Not on purpose.... You know I didn't mean anything I said."

She turned to face him. Her voice was exasperated. "It's not *me,* you idiot. It's yourself you're being mean to. What are you trying to do? Punish the legs that are gone?"

There. She'd said it. She waited for him to throw her out again. But he didn't. He gave a long sigh and reached for her. She put both arms around him and let him bury his head against her shoulder.

"You're the only one who can talk to me, Angie. You're the only one who can make me see myself." His voice cracked, and her blouse grew wet with his tears. "Don't leave me, Angie. I need you."

She held him there and whispered to him until he began to take long, deep breaths. Then she made her voice come out as calm and sure as she could. "I'm not going to leave you, Con. But that's not enough. You have to do your part. You have to try, Con."

When he answered her, his voice was muffled, but she could hear his words clearly. "OK, Angie. If it means that much to you, I'll try."

11
MR. ERICKSON

It was a hot summer. It seemed to Angie that it was the hottest she had ever known. Each day she and Caro worked mornings. In the afternoons, Angie bought a single flower from Old Lu to take to Con. Then she went to the hospital and stayed until visiting hours were over.

Most of Angie's visits were hard ones. Even after Con started using the wheelchair and going to therapy, no miracles happened.

One day, a few weeks after the accident, she had almost reached the end of the hall when she heard voices coming out of Con's room. A man was talking. She heard Con, too, but she almost didn't believe it.

Con was laughing!

Angie stepped cautiously into the room and saw Con propped up on two large pillows. There was a big grin on his face. Whoever that man sitting in the chair was, she didn't like him. It wasn't fair that he should make Con act like his old self in one single visit, while she had been trying day after day.

"Come on in, Angie. Look who's here. Mr. Frickson, this is Angie."

The man had his back to her. He got up slowly from his chair and turned so that Angie could see his face. She didn't recognize him, but she knew that Mr. Erickson was the athletic coach from Con's school.

"Hello, Angie. I've heard a lot about you."

She held out her hand. "How do you do."

"Mr. Erickson's been telling me some funny stories about his experiences," Con said. "But, listen to this, Angie. He really thinks I'll be able to walk again. They have been trying to talk to me about it in therapy, but I ... wouldn't listen."

Mr. Erickson smiled at Angie. "Artificial legs aren't what they used to be. They're much better. There's no reason why Con can't walk and finish his education ... and have a career."

He went to the door; then he stopped and looked at Con. "Just remember what I told you, Con ... about trusting. You have a lot of friends, but there's one who's with you twenty-four hours a day. The Lord isn't going to give you your own legs back, but he'll give you the strength to get along without them."

He lifted a hand and smiled at them both. Then he turned and walked down the hall. There was something unusual about the way he moved.

Angie noticed it, but not for long. She was too busy being mad at him. Artificial legs! She knew what they were. Stumps of wood that made hollow sounds on the sidewalk. She had seen them on an old man who used to come to the mission. All the kids had laughed at him. Angie shivered, remembering Stumpy Sam.

Oh, no! Con wasn't going to be like that. If he had to stay in a wheelchair, at least he'd look ... well, dignifed. And she was the one who would take care of him.

"Hey, Angie! What're you looking so glum about? Didn't you hear what the man said? I don't have to stay in that contraption forever."

He pointed to the corner of the room near the head of his bed where the collapsible wheelchair was folded flat against the wall.

"What's the matter with your wheelchair?" she asked. "Lots of people use wheelchairs."

"Not if they have another choice. Listen, Angie. I'm not trying to be funny or anything. But I really mean it when I say I'm not going to take this lying down. Not when there's a chance of standing up."

Standing up on wooden legs! Angie stuffed the flower in Flo's vase. "He's not a doctor, is he?"

"Of course not. But he knows a lot about artificial legs. He has one himself."

Mr. Erickson? Angie didn't believe it. Then she remembered the careful way he had gotten up from the chair and his slow, unhurried walk down the hall. But he didn't use crutches.

"He doesn't walk like Stumpy Sam," she said.

Con began to laugh. "Is that why you want to keep me in a wheelchair? So I won't walk like Stumpy Sam? Angie, I'm not talking about wooden legs. I'm talking about things called prostheses. Artificial limbs. It's a science, Angie. Dr. Stinson says it's really possible to make arms and legs. They're not skin and bone, and they're not as good as the real things. But neither are false teeth—and millions of people get along with those."

Angie didn't answer him. Con was looking at her with a puzzled expression on his face. "Hey!" he said. "What is this? Can't you smile?"

Angie wished that she could talk about her feelings the way Con could. "I ... thought he was getting your hopes up for nothing," she said. "You and I ... we were doing OK, Con. I don't mind pushing you in a wheelchair."

It wasn't the truth, and she knew it. Angie was down in the mouth because she was jealous. Jealous of Mr. Erickson, who had made Con smile. She looked away from Con. He always had a way of figuring out what she was thinking.

It was too late. His face softened, and he reached for her hand. "You've been doing great, Angie. You're the one who has kept me going. But now it's time for me to get my act together. Something's happened to me, Angie. I can't explain it yet. But I feel good. I really feel like I'm going to make it."

He paused. "You do want me to walk again, don't you? You want us to be together, the way we planned? Hey, Angie! Look at me! Do you feel different now ... because I don't have any legs?"

How could she tell him what was inside of her? Of course she felt different. She wanted to take care of him now. She wanted to make it up to him.

Angie couldn't make herself tell him all these things. But he was waiting for an answer, and she could tell him what he wanted to hear.

"I feel the same way I always have ... about you, Con." She could say that much. She loved Con.

He looked relieved. "Don't worry, Angie. I'm going to get out of here. I'm still going to get that scholarship. It won't be an athletic one, and I may have to work a little harder, but I'll get it. I'll pave the road for us, Angie, even if I have to do it on my hands and knees."

Then he started laughing.

"What's so funny?" she asked.

"I am. I can't seem to remember. I won't have to crawl, Angie. I'm going to walk!"

Angie laughed with him. She didn't want him to know that she had decided not to believe a word that Mr. Erickson had said.

12
ONE STEP AT A TIME

During the next weeks Angie realized that Con was a different person. Oh, he still looked the same, but there was something about him. Even in his wheelchair, Angie thought he seemed bigger.

One day he came whirring down the hallway in his chair and found her sitting by his bed. This wasn't the first time he had been out of his room when she arrived.

"I'm sorry, Angie," he said. "I didn't mean to be so late, but ..." Then he began to smile.

She smiled back. It was good to see Con looking happy. "What is it?" she asked.

"Tomorrow you can come with me to therapy. It's OK for you to visit. You can see everything we do in there, Angie. You can finally see for yourself."

Then he reached out and gave her hand a squeeze. "Oh, Angie!" he said, laughing, as if he had a secret. "I can't wait until tomorrow!"

But Angie could wait. She dreaded going to that place. The next afternoon she walked so slowly on her way to the hospital that she got there a lot later than usual. Con was sitting in his wheelchair in the hallway, looking impatient.

"I've been waiting for you," he said. "Come on. Let's get going." He gave the wheels a push that sent him rolling ahead of her down the hall. She hurried along behind him and tried not to feel irritated. Con had always let her push him in that chair. Con scooted ahead of her again and led the way to the end of the hall where swinging double doors had been propped open to reveal a large room.

Angie came closer and looked in. This place wasn't what she had expected at all. It was like a gymnasium.

Con went through the doorway and motioned for her to follow. "I want you to meet someone," he said. "Angie, this is Joe Sullivan. He's a physical therapist. He's also a pretty good friend."

Joe smiled. "Glad to meet you, Angie. Have you ever visited here before?"

Angie shook her head. "I wasn't sure I wanted to come. I didn't think it would look like this. I . . . I'm not sure what I thought."

Joe nodded. "That's the way it is with most people. Some of them are even afraid to come." He nodded toward Con. "We had a terrible time getting him in here. Now we can't get him out. Come on and have a look around."

They walked slowly through the room. Con seemed to know everybody, and it took a long time to stop and talk with each person. Some were lying on long tables, being massaged. Some were working with machines, pushing . . . pulling . . . strengthening muscles. A few were walking very slowly along short ramps with steel handgrips along the sides.

They made a complete circuit and came back to the door. Con had stayed behind to talk to a friend, and Joe and Angie were standing together, waiting. "Well, what do you think?" Joe asked.

Angie hesitated. "How can they be so happy when they've lost so much?"

Joe looked thoughtful. "We try to tell people that they're still whole on the inside, and that's where it counts. That's what Con is learning, Angie. He's finding out he can be independent again."

"But he didn't deserve this," Angie said.

"That's not the point. Life isn't a free ride, Angie, and it's no good feeling cheated when things don't go your way. You just have to pull yourself together and do the best you can with what you've got." He leaned over closer. "Con is finding out that he's a lot stronger than he thought he was. That's the first step to independence. And that's what Con needs most of all."

Angie thought about that all the way back to Con's room. She didn't try to push him this time, but watched him wheel himself along. He did it easily. Con didn't need pushing anymore.

Then what did Con need? And what was he doing about it? She had walked through the therapy room and seen all the equipment. But she hadn't seen Con using it. What did he do in there? What was happening to make him so happy?

She stood in front of his wheelchair. "Con, when you go to therapy, what do you do?"

"Lots of different exercises." He hesitated. "Especially arm exercises. You have to have strong arms to handle a wheelchair."

"So I noticed." She took a deep breath. "Con, have you given up trying to walk?"

He was really avoiding her now. "No ... no, of course not. A thing like that takes a long time, that's all. Hey, look what time it is. Visiting hours are almost over."

Angie stared at him. He acted as if he wanted her to leave. But he wasn't mad at her. She could see the laughter in his eyes when he looked up and said, "See you tomorrow, Angie? Same time?"

She nodded. "If you're sure you want me to come."

This time the laughter bubbled right out of him. He grinned and took her hand. "Oh, I want you to come all right. You can't miss tomorrow."

The next afternoon, Angie walked into Con's room

and found his bed empty. There wasn't anything to do but sit and wait. She closed her eyes and listened.

She heard the nurse's voice instead, right outside the door. "Wait a minute, I'll see if she's here yet."

Angie opened her eyes and looked up at a white-capped head, poking around the edge of the doorway. "She's here, all right," the nurse said. "Will you step out here into the hallway a minute?" she asked.

Angie got up and followed her out of the room. The nurse just pointed. Angie followed her finger.

Con was about halfway down the hall holding onto the railings of one of those three-sided steel frames. He was standing. And he was smiling at her.

Con standing! Angie closed her eyes, then looked again. She must be losing her mind. Con was wearing a blue T-shirt, and ...

She looked quickly to where his legs should have been and saw the long pants. He was wearing Levis. There were brown shoes on his ... No, that wasn't possible. For a second she felt a little dizzy.

Then Con did something she would never forget. He took a careful step forward, than another, moving his left leg and then his right. He was walking. Con was standing up and walking. He was also laughing.

The hallway was becoming crowded with people: nurses in white uniforms and doctors in green scrub suits. The doorways were filled with all the patients who were able to get out of bed to see Con walk. Angie knew they were there, and she knew they were clapping and cheering, but she really didn't see them. She didn't hear a thing except the sound of Con's voice saying over and over, "I'm coming, Angie."

She waited for him until he stood in front of her, just like Con had always stood—tall and strong.

She couldn't say anything for a long time; her throat was tight, and she was close to sobbing. She watched as the nurse helped him onto the bed and raised the back until he was sitting up against the pillows. Then she wiped her eyes and looked at him.

"You walked," she finally said. "I saw you walk!"

"I've been doing it for quite a while, but I didn't want you to see me until I was sure I wouldn't fall on my face. I've been waiting to surprise you, Angie."

He reached down and gave the shapes beneath his pants a friendly pat. "These things are only temporary. They're like long posts with rubber feet.... How about that? Now I can stub my toe and it won't hurt! Do you want to see them?"

Angie smiled weakly. "Not right now, thanks."

Con grinned. "I didn't want to see them, either. Not at first. But now they don't bother me at all." His voice quickened with excitement. "Just wait until I get the real things, Angie. Dr. Stinson says I can learn to walk quicker, because I still have one knee of my own."

He pointed to the walker. "I'll get rid of that thing as soon as I get my balance. Then I'll be on crutches for a while."

Angie felt like she needed to be quiet so she could think, but Con was pulling at her hand, demanding her attention. "Didn't you hear me, Angie? When I'm ready to throw away the crutches, they'll let me walk with a cane. Someday I can throw that away, too.

"And listen to this. I don't have to stay in the hospital all that time. I can go home in two more weeks, Angie. I can start school in September.

"Listen, Angie. I haven't told anybody else, but I want you to know what's been happening to me. After the accident, I used to lie here and pretend it wasn't true. But I couldn't keep that up very long, because I kept looking down and seeing that two big pieces of me were gone.

"So I tried something else. I kept remembering that neon sign over the mission that says PRAYER CHANGES THINGS, and I decided that I wanted it to change me. I prayed every night, Angie. I spent a lot of time telling God what I wanted him to do for me.

"Give me back my legs, Lord. I won't ever ask you for another thing, if you'll just give them back. But nothing happened. Not one darned thing.

"I felt worse and worse, until one night I couldn't sleep at all. Every time I closed my eyes, it seemed like I was sitting at the bottom of a deep well, with no rope to climb up on. I felt so low that I didn't care what happened to me. There wasn't anything to do but give up.

"I said it right out loud: 'OK, God, my legs are gone, and I know I'm not going to grow any new ones. So let's try it your way. Just show me what you want me to do.'

"It seemed like somebody let down a rope and pulled me up where I could see daylight again. I opened my eyes, and it really was daylight. The sun was coming in through the window, and the darkness just drained out of me.

"I had given up, Angie, but I didn't feel like a quitter anymore. I felt like I was starting all over again ... like I had decided to take another chance on life."

Angie was beginning to feel pretty uncomfortable. Con was smiling at her, waiting for her to say something, and she didn't have any idea what to say. That was the trouble with Con. He thought, and then he had to put his thoughts into words. He was good at that. But when he finished, he expected Angie to say something back. Usually she said all the wrong things.

This time she decided to play it safe. "You always make sense," she told him, and she squeezed his hand hard. But, inside, she was confused. Suddenly she wanted to go home. She had a lot of things to think about.

"One step at a time," he told her. "We're going to make it, Angie." He smiled tiredly. "I can go almost anywhere on these legs." Then he put his head on the pillow and closed his eyes.

Angie closed hers, too. She remembered when he had said those same words on a rooftop, about a million years ago.

She waited until she was sure he was sleeping, then tiptoed out of the room. She went quickly down the hall to the elevator and pushed the button. She was outside on the hospital steps when she remembered something Con had said. He was coming home in two weeks. Home to Bundy Street.

That's what Dr. Stinson had told him. But Dr. Stinson didn't know that Con's home was a deserted apartment on the second floor. He didn't know about Orly. Or about Con's mother who didn't care.

She also knew what happened to minors who were deserted by their parents. They got put into foster homes. She had to find a place for Con to live. They would take him away. She'd never see him again. Con didn't even know it, she thought, but he still needed her.

She kept thinking about what Con had said. She had always connected God with that statue of George Washington on top of the mission. She had always thought that believing in him was a little like believing in the president. You knew he existed, but you never had a chance to get acquainted.

Con had made it all sound different. He acted almost like he had really been introduced and had a chance to shake hands. God might be on Con's side. She wasn't going to argue about that. But she was going to have to find a place for Con to live.

Angie pulled her shoulders back and walked a little faster. She wasn't going to be a quitter, either. You had to be a fighter to survive in this world, and that's what she intended to be.

She just wished she could bury the thought at the edge of her mind that kept telling her that she was sinking into a deep well.

13
THE LOCKED DOOR

When Angie came up the front steps of the apartment building, she saw that the front door was ajar. Voices were coming from just inside. She didn't mean to eavesdrop, but she couldn't seem to help it. Tony and her mother were talking together.

"I've got to get the girls out of here, Tony."

"I know how you feel, Evelyn. But how do you think you're going to manage that? Moving takes money."

Angie stopped on the top step. They couldn't leave Bundy Street now. Not when Con needed a home. Then she heard Tony's voice again.

"Evelyn ..."

Just one word. That was all he said. It hung on the air like a question mark until her mother wiped it away with a single sentence.

"Tony, I ... have an aunt back East."

Angie knew who that would be. Her name was Aunt Marth, and she lived in Massachusetts. Every Christmas she sent them a box that contained ugly, black, hand-knit stockings.

Tony laughed, but it wasn't a happy sound. "Ha!" he said. "You've told me about her, all right. Isn't she the one who wouldn't let you come home after Frank died?"

Angie stood absolutely still. Now she was listening on

purpose. Frank was her father's name. But he hadn't died. Tony had the story all wrong.

"Aunt Martha never approved of Frank," her mother answered. "The hard part is that she was right. When things got tough for him, he just walked out on us. She knew he would never come back, and I knew it, too. Just the same, it was a shock when I heard he was killed in an accident. Tony, I ... never told the girls. I suppose I'll have to someday."

For a few seconds, Angie didn't hear another thing. Her ears were ringing, and she had to concentrate hard to catch her mother's next words.

"Aunt Martha said she never wanted to see me again, because I had disobeyed her, but she would be willing to see that the girls got a proper upbringing."

Angie felt a cold chill go right down her back. She would never live with Aunt Martha. Never! But the worst thing was that her mother had lied to her ... and to Caro, too. The old dream flashed through her head and disappeared like a burned-out light bulb—all in one big flash.

"I wrote to Aunt Martha today, Tony. I asked her to let them come and stay. They don't have a chance here on Bundy Street."

"Evelyn ..." Tony sounded like he had a sore throat. "Families should be together."

"We will be together as soon as I get a better job. I need to go back to school, Tony. I can rent a single room, and work nights and study days. I used to type pretty well. All I need is a little shorthand. Later, I'll get a better place to live, and I'll send for the girls, and ..."

"Wait a minute. ... You're not thinking straight, because you're upset. You said you were miserable growing up in your aunt's house. How do you think your girls will feel?"

Her voice was stiff when she answered. It was the same voice she used on Angie when she didn't want to talk about something anymore. "I know what's best for them, and it's not living here. Anyway, it's too late. I've already written the letter."

Tony's voice was so low Angie could hardly hear him. "Have you thought what this will do to Con?"

There was a long silence. "I can't help it," her mother finally said.

Angie bit the inside of her cheek. How she hated being thirteen. If she were only a few years older, she could ... She was so angry she didn't realize that the talking had stopped. Suddenly, her mother and Tony were standing on the porch, looking at her.

"How long have you been listening, young lady?" her mother demanded.

"Long enough," she said defiantly.

"Listen, Angie." Her mother's voice softened. "We need to talk. I want you to understand ..."

Angie shook her head. "If you want to get rid of Caro and me, I guess there isn't anything we can do about it, is there? But maybe you can tell me where Con is going to live when we're gone." Her voice rose. "They're letting him out of the hospital in two weeks. You didn't know that, did you? When they find out he doesn't even have an address, they'll put him in a foster home, and you won't even care!"

She was yelling. She was being rude and horrible, and she was glad. She took a deep breath and got ready for a whole lot more. But Tony stepped in and ruined the whole thing.

"They already know the whole story," Tony told her. "Listen, Angie, you don't have to worry about a foster home, because Tony's Deli is the foster home they're sending Con to. He wanted it to be a surprise."

Angie looked from one of them to the other. She knew she ought to feel glad, but she didn't. They'd done this behind her back. It wasn't a surprise. It was just plain sneaky. She hated them for it.

"I've had enough surprises for one day," she said. Then she stepped around Tony and walked past her mother without another word.

"Just one minute ..." her mother began.

"Leave her alone, Evelyn," Tony said. His voice was tired, and he sounded discouraged. "You go on to work so you won't be late."

Angie kicked the door shut so she couldn't hear their voices. The apartment was empty.

She went into the kitchen and stared at the refrigerator, remembering what her mother had said to her before she left for the hospital. "If you don't pick up some powdered milk on your way home, there won't be any for dinner tonight."

Well, she hadn't, and there wasn't. So what? Angie reached into the cupboard and took out a jar of instant coffee. She would make a cup, and she would drink it black. Nobody was going to stop her.

She opened the jar and measured out two heaping spoonfuls. Then she boiled water and poured it into the cup. The coffee was strong and bitter and so hot it burned her tongue.

She sat at the table and stared straight ahead. She felt as if she were wearing somebody else's glasses. There were colors and shapes in front of her, but she didn't see them clearly. Gradually, one of the colors grew brighter and took shape. She forced her eyes to focus on it.

It was the red plastic geranium in the kitchen window. It was a fake, she thought, hating it. "Fake!" she said out loud. "Fake, like Con's legs. Fake, like everything else around this place."

She pounded her fist hard on the table. The coffee sloshed out of the cup and made a dark pool on the shiny Formica surface. Angie didn't bother to clean it up. She got up and dumped the contents of her cup into the sink. A dark, oily scum formed over the cold, white enamel.

Angie looked at it and began to cry. She didn't make a sound, but the tears ran down her face and into her mouth. She reached up for the red geranium with both hands and pulled it from the pot. Tiny clods of dirt exploded into the sink and mixed with the wet coffee scum.

Angie stared at them. Boy, was that funny! Her mother had planted that fake geranium in real dirt. She walked to the wastebasket and dropped it in. Then she reached in with her hands and buried it beneath the other trash.

Angie went into the bathroom and washed her hands and face. When Caro came back from Flo's, Angie took enough meat out of the refrigerator to make two hamburger patties.

Then she watched television with Caro and listened to her talk about everything she had done that day. They pulled the bed out so Caro could lie down while she watched television. She wasn't tired, she told Angie. But before it was dark outside, she had closed her eyes.

Angie turned the television down to a murmur, watched Caro for a minute to make sure she wasn't pretending, and then slipped quietly out the door.

She knew exactly where she was going. Angie could breathe best up on the roof. It was quiet up there. She had a lot to think about.

She tried to empty her mind of everything, especially the things that had happened that afternoon. She tried to tip her brain over and let everything run out, just like she had dumped the bitter, black coffee from her cup into the sink. But no matter how hard she tried, there was always some scum left in the bottom.

Why did she resent Con's independence? Why had she been so hateful to Tony? Why couldn't she try to understand what her mother had done?

Angie had never wished for a father as hard as she

wished for one right now. Everything would be different if she had a father to talk to. She could go to him when she was in trouble. She wouldn't feel like she had to figure out everything all by herself.

Angie closed her eyes and willed the old dream back one more time. She made her father walk down the street and up the front steps. She made him tap three times on the door. In her mind, Angie stood there with her hands sweating and her heart beating hard. Then she reached out and turned the knob as she always did.

But this time nothing happened. The door was locked. Angie twisted the knob and pulled hard, but it wouldn't open. He was there, but he couldn't get in. She heard him knocking on the other side of the door. She didn't want him to be a stranger.

"Father ..." she called.

She opened her eyes quickly and looked around. She was alone on the rooftop. The voice she had heard was her own. She had said the words out loud, and no one had answered her. But for a few short seconds, Angie had felt like someone really was there. Someone who could help her figure things out or throw her a rope if she fell into a deep well.

That's what Con had said. But Con hadn't been talking about her father. He had been talking about God.

Could God be a father? There was a prayer that started out like that. *Our Father, who art in heaven ...* Angie had never really thought of God like that. He'd always seemed more like the George Washington statue over the mission.

A real father would be someone who was there when you needed him. He would be warm and loving. He would never give up, even when you did.

What was it that Con had said? You can give up without being a quitter. Angie didn't see how. But the way she felt tonight, giving up seemed like the only thing left for her to do.

She leaned her head back against the face of the wall and closed her eyes. She sat very still. "OK," she said out loud. "I give up."

She kept her eyes closed and waited. She waited for about fifteen minutes. Con had said it was like a miracle for him. But Angie didn't feel a thing.

Finally, she said it louder, just in case God hadn't heard her. "I ... GIVE ... UP!"

But nothing happened. Nothing at all.

Angie stood up and stamped her foot. "What is it you want me to do? What do you expect, anyway? Do you want me to get down on my knees and tell you how helpless I am? Well, I am not helpless. So how do you like that?"

Nobody answered. Angie hadn't really expected a booming voice out of the sky. But she had hoped for some kind of a sign. Maybe she had made God mad. That might be the reason nothing happened.

But Angie knew that wasn't true. The real reason was that stupid locked door inside her head. No matter how hard she pulled on it, she didn't know how to make it open.

She looked up at the stars. It seemed more likely to her that God would be there than down on Bundy Street. "Show me how to open the door," she whispered. "Please show me how."

The night winds blew across the rooftop. But they didn't tell her a thing. Briefly, like a candle flickers when it's about to go out, she saw a light in the old abandoned house at the end of the street.

Angie shivered. She must have imagined that. Nobody ever went in that place. She walked slowly across the roof, climbed down to the narrow balcony at the back of the house, and went through the door into the room at the top. There weren't any answers for her tonight.

She went down the stairs to the front door, opened it, and stepped out onto the front porch. The long, tangled weed that had been growing there for several weeks had twined, like ivy, all the way up one of the mortuary columns. Angie looked at it closely; then she reached out to touch a long, milky-white bud. It broke off and lay in her palm.

The bud felt soft and strange against her skin, like cool silk. She began to pull it apart, starting with the tissuey folds at the tip. It tore, revealing a deep, bright purple center: a five-pointed star connected by delicate lavender webbing.

Angie stared at it a second; then she reached out and dropped it over the edge of the porch. There was a stickiness still on her palm when she opened the front door and went back inside. It was the only door she was able to open. It was her own address.

14
GUIDELINES

In the morning, when Angie opened the front door of the apartment building, Jessica was sitting on the front steps. She hadn't seen Jessica since that day at the skating rink. The day when Jessica had called Bundy Street a slum, and all Angie's troubles had started. Jessica was sitting like she always did with her chin on her hands and her elbows on her knees. Angie clicked the door shut and watched Jessica turn around.

"I heard about Con. I ... thought I might go see him in the hospital." Jessica cleared her throat. "I was just wondering if ... he'd want to see me or not."

Angie glanced at her. Jessica kept pulling her hair back behind her ears. Angie wished she would quit it. It was making her nervous.

Jessica looked at her and put her hands in her lap. "You don't think Con ran away with Took because of what I said ... do you, Angie?"

Angie was startled. "Because of what you said?" Nothing Jessica said would ever matter to Con.

"You know—about Bundy Street being a slum." Jessica turned her head away.

Then Angie saw Jessica bite her lip. She couldn't believe it. Jessica Smith, who thought she was better than anybody, was about to lose her cool.

"I can't stand it anymore, Angie," she said. "Ever

since the accident, I've been thinking about that day. I keep wondering if … any of it was my fault."

Her voice squeaked like a mouse in a trap, and she buried her face in her lap. Angie had never liked Jessica very much, and she couldn't honestly say that she liked her any better now. But she had to admit that she felt sorry for her. Angie knew exactly how she felt. She waited a minute; then she reached out a hand and reluctantly put it on Jessica's shoulder.

"Hey, Jessica," she said. "You don't need to feel that way. It really wasn't your fault. It wasn't anybody's fault."

Except Took's. Mentally, Angie subtracted his name from her list of anybodies. As far as she was concerned, he didn't classify.

Jessica looked up. "You're just telling me that to make me feel better," she said.

"For pete's sake, Jess. Why would I do a thing like that? I don't even like you."

Jessica brightened. "That's right, you don't. So I guess I can believe you." She looked at Angie a minute. "I don't like you, either. But I don't not like you as much as I used to."

Angie nodded. "I know what you mean." She suddenly felt generous. "I think Con might like it if you came by the hospital," she told her.

Jessica pulled her hair back behind her ears again and stood up. She pulled a handkerchief out of her pocket and wiped her eyes. Then she pointed at the climbing vine. "Who planted that?" she asked.

Angie stared at it. It looked as if it had grown several inches since yesterday, and it was full of buds, like the one she had picked last night. "Nobody planted it. It's just some kind of weed," she said.

Jessica shook her head firmly. "That's no weed. It looks like a morning-glory vine. The flowers last one day, but they only open up when the sun shines. Gee, Angie, they make lots of seeds. You could have morning glories all over Bundy Street by next year."

"Jessica, I've never seen a real flower on this street ... except for the ones in Old Lu's cart."

Jessica shrugged and started down the steps. "That's probably because nobody planted any." She walked a few steps; then she turned and came back. "I almost forgot to tell you. Took's mother is looking for him."

"Well, she must not worry about him too much. He's been missing since the night of the accident."

Jessica shrugged. "You know how it is. Took isn't the kind of person to check in every night. But after a couple of weeks his mother began to think it was kind of strange. She'll give him a few more days, and then she's going to report him to the police."

Angie looked at Jessica carefully. She seemed to know an awful lot about Took. If she was telling the truth, he was about to become a missing person after all.

"I've gotta go," Jessica said. She stood on the sidewalk looking at Angie. "See you around?"

"Sure," Angie answered. "Why not?"

Then she watched Jessica walk down Bundy Street towards Chico's corner. The door slammed behind her, and Caro came out on the porch and gave her a nudge. "You ready to go to Flo's?" she asked.

"It's too early. Anyway, I have to talk to Tony. Why don't you go on ahead?"

Angie knew why Caro was in a hurry. Flo had put her in charge of all the potted plants at Maria's. She must have a green thumb, Flo had explained, because the plants were growing.

Caro wasn't satisfied with just gardening at Flo's. A few days ago Angie had seen her walking up and down the street with water-filled milk cartons, pouring a little liquid on each dusty, wire-protected tree.

Angie leaned over, curiously, and looked at the base of the morning-glory vine. Just as she had thought. Caro had watered that, too. The crack in the concrete was still damp. No wonder the silly vine was growing.

A chattering noise across the street made her look toward the Deli. Tony had pulled a ladder onto the sidewalk, and he was beginning to wash the display window at the front of his store. Bandit's rope was looped around the leg of the ladder. The little monkey perched on the warm sidewalk and rubbed his tiny hands in the soapy water.

Angie got up and started slowly across the street. She had to talk to Tony, but she wasn't exactly sure what she was going to say.

"Hi!" It seemed a safe enough way to start.

"Morning, Angie." Tony kept right on washing.

Angie reached over and scratched Bandit behind his little ears. He gave a shriek and jumped to the ledge. Then he looked at Tony and began copying him, rubbing the glass with his wet paws.

"That window doesn't look dirty to me," Angie said. "What are you washing it for?"

Tony looked over his shoulder. "Do you wait until you're good and dirty before you take a bath?" He rubbed hard on a smudge. "Clean windows make me feel good. Maybe someday the rest of Bundy Street will take the hint."

Angie leaned against the doorway and watched him. "It'll take more than clean windows to change things around here," she said.

He climbed down from the stepladder. To her surprise he held up his index finger and shook it in her face. "Clean windows are a good start," he said. "And washing them is better than complaining."

He turned around and swung the ladder up under one arm and picked up the bucket of water in the other hand. For a second, Bandit was free. The little monkey headed next door, straight for the sunbather, who spent most of every warm day in front of the mission. Bandit landed, with a plop, right on his lap and began to wash the man's face with his soapy paws.

"Help!" the man yelled. "Somebody get this monster off me!"

Angie had never seen the man look alive before.

But he looked alive now. He jumped straight up in the air. His eyes and mouth were open, and he was waving his arms around over his head. Bandit hung tightly to the man's jacket.

Tony dropped everything and ran to the rescue. "Cut that out!" he yelled. "You're scaring my monkey!"

Bandit gave a jump and landed in Tony's arms. The bucket of soapy water had spilled, and a pool began to form in front of the mission. The sunbather pointed at the wet sidewalk and began to shout.

"Now look what you've done! How do you expect me to sit out here?"

Tony calmly lifted up his index finger. He was getting pretty handy with it, Angie thought, as he thrust it right in the sunbather's face. "I don't expect you to sit at all. Now that you've shown us how fast you can move, why don't you stay on your feet and do something useful?"

The sunbather looked uncomfortable.

"You've got *time*, haven't you?" Tony pointed to the cracked stucco and the gold paint peeling from the statue. "Just look at that! A little paint and plaster would fix all of it ... if anybody cared enough to try."

The sunbather looked down at his shoes. "Where would I get paint and plaster?"

"Inside!" Tony's voice thundered. "In the storeroom off the kitchen. I donated it myself when George Washington first began to peel!"

The man stepped back, looked up at the statue, and stared. "Is that George Washington?" he asked.

Angie and Tony left him standing there. They went into the Deli, Tony going first, with the ladder and Bandit, and Angie following, carrying the empty bucket.

She didn't say anything for a while. Just sat on a stool

and watched as Tony got ready to open up the store. He was acting different this morning, banging things around and slamming cupboards, like he was mad at somebody. She wished he would look at her, but he just went about his business. Angie slipped from her stool and went to the little round table that Tony kept for customers who wanted to sit down.

The table was in a corner that was decorated with posters of Italy on the walls. Between two bright posters was a black frame. Behind the glass were some words written in heavy black ink. Angie leaned forward to read them. "I went to the woods because I wished to live deliberately . . . and not, when I came to die, discover that I had not lived."

Beneath the words was the author's name. Thoreau. They had studied him in school. She read the words again. Was that the way Tony felt? Did he want to go and live in the woods like Thoreau had?

She turned around to ask him and found that he was already standing right behind her. He put his arm around her shoulders and she saw, with relief, that he was the old Tony—the one she could talk to—not an angry stranger.

She wanted to say she was sorry about the awful way she had acted last night. She wanted to tell him she was glad that Con was coming here to live. But she didn't.

"Oh, Tony, why did my mother lie to me. Why did she tell me my father had to go away? I've been waiting, Tony. I thought he would be coming back."

"Angie, your mother didn't want you to be hurt."

Angie gave a little laugh. "She doesn't want me at all. Or Caro, either. We're in her way. That's why she wants us to go to live with Aunt Martha."

"You know that's not true. Your mother loves you both. She's just worried, because of what happened to Con—and because she thinks your Aunt Martha can give you a good home and things your mother can never afford."

"If my mother doesn't want us, we won't stay in her way. But we're not going to Massachusetts, either. Caro and I are ... running away."

It wasn't true, and she knew it. But she felt better because she had said it.

Tony sighed and sat down hard on one of the little white metal chairs; then he motioned her into the other one. "There isn't any such thing as running away, Angie. Wherever we go, we take our problems with us." He pointed to the words on the wall. "That's what Thoreau was talking about. We all have to stop somewhere and take a stand on what we believe in. We have to live on purpose, Angie. Deliberately."

"But ... things happen, Tony. Things you don't plan on. How can you live on purpose when your life is all messed up?"

"You just look around you and face facts, and then you see what you can do to make them better."

"You mean like praying about them? I tried it, and it doesn't work for me."

He leaned back in his chair. "I'll bet it doesn't ... if you only pray for things."

She looked at him suspiciously. "What are you getting at?"

"Prayer changes people, Angie. And people can work together to change things. That's what living on purpose is all about."

He reached out and took hold of her hands. "Look, honey, things don't always turn out the way we plan them. Man's free will is a great gift, but sometimes it gets us into trouble. That's why we need a lot of guidance. It's there, if we just ask for it. It helps us make responsible decisions ... Angie, it keeps us from running away."

Angie shrugged. "So, what am I supposed to do now? Make the best of Massachusetts?"

He looked at her a long time. "You're not in Massachusetts yet. You might try making the best of Bundy Street. Now wait a minute, Angie! Don't make a long face like that. Bundy Street does have possibilities. Just because part of a city grows old, that doesn't mean it has to become a slum. There are lots of good things about Bundy Street. Just look how people have shown they care about Con."

"But how can you change the rest of it? The dirty sidewalks, and cracks in the walls, and the ..."

Tony held up his hand for silence. "Listen!"

There was a strange, scraping sound coming from somewhere outside, on the front side of the building. Tony went quickly to the doorway.

"Come here, Angie," he called.

Angie stood beside him and stared up at the gold statue. The sunbather had propped a tall ladder against the front of the building and was standing on it, while he chipped flaking gold paint away from George Washington's coat. On the ledge beside him sat two cans of paint and a large, thick brush.

"Angie, my girl, you start with something small ... like washing a window. Then you give a few gentle hints ..."

Angie had to smile. She didn't think Tony's hints to the sunbather had been so gentle. Then she found the courage to ask him a question.

"What were you so mad about this morning, Tony?"

His mustache twitched when he answered. "I was mad at your mother, Angie, for wanting to leave. And I was mad at myself for not having the courage to tell her how I feel ... about all of you."

Angie stared at him. How did he feel? She waited for him to tell her, but his mustache twitched again, and he turned without another word and went inside to wait on a customer.

15
CHAIN REACTION

Angie thought a lot about what Tony had said. She worked at Flo's and visited Con and came back to Bundy Street and thought some more. She didn't want to ruin the hope by putting it into words before she was sure it was true. Tony and her mother? Just thinking about it made her happy and scared at the same time. What if Tony never mentioned it again? What if they all moved away?

By the next morning she had decided what she was going to do. She was going to tell Caro about Aunt Martha. Then the two of them were going to start a chain reaction, even if they had to do all the reacting themselves. They had to show their mother that Bundy Street wasn't a slum. They had to make her want to stay here, with them ... with Tony ... and with Con.

Angie waited until she and Caro were alone that night. "I have something important to tell you," she said. "It's about Aunt Martha. We may go and live with her. Mom already wrote a letter, asking if it's all right."

Caro squinted her eyes and looked at Angie through the slits. "You're making that up."

"No, I'm not. She really wrote it. I heard her tell Tony. She's afraid if we stay here, something bad will happen to us, like it did to Con."

Caro turned white. "It's a dump all right. I used to

want to leave, but now ..."

"I know." She nodded. "The place has its good points after all. Even if it didn't, I wouldn't want to go and live with Aunt Martha, would you?"

Caro looked scared. She shook her head.

"Then there's only one thing to do," Angie told her.

"You mean, run away?"

"No, silly! I said that to Tony, but I didn't mean it. You have to figure out what to do about your problems right where you find them, and our problem is Bundy Street. Listen, Caro, Jessica said that weed on the front porch is really a flower that makes lots of seeds. She said they could spread, and we might have flowers all over Bundy Street.

"Well, I laughed at her and told her I'd never seen any real flowers here, except the ones for sale on Old Lu's cart. You know what she told me? She said that's just because nobody ever planted any."

Caro pursed her lips. "You said Jessica was stupid."

Angie sighed. "She's not quite as stupid as I thought. She was right. Bundy Street is the way it is, because nobody ever planted any seeds before."

"You mean idea seeds," Caro exclaimed. "Like cleaning things up, and ... watering the trees ... and washing the Deli window."

Angie nodded. "Some of them are already starting to sprout. George Washington is getting a new coat of gold paint."

"Oh, Angie. Do you think we can clean the street up before Con comes home? We only have two weeks."

In the morning, Angie took her mother's broom; then she went next door and borrowed Flo's for Caro to use. They started on opposite sides of the street: Caro in front of Pete's Parking and Angie in front of the deserted house on the corner. There was something about that place that bothered Angie, especially since she had seen a light flickering in one of the windows. When she came to Flo's, the door opened, and Flo's curler-adorned head stuck out.

"What are you kids up to?" she demanded.

"We're sweeping. It's supposed to give people ideas. You know, get them interested in cleaning up Bundy Street."

Flo looked puzzled. "For pity's sake!" she exclaimed. She closed the door, but Angie could see her through the front window of Maria's, standing in the middle of the room.

Angie swept past the apartments, moving a little slower now. By the time she had finished the front of Hoang Chou's, her arms ached, and she felt like sitting down. When she reached Chico's, the palms of her hands were burning, and the dust from the sidewalk was making her sneeze.

Across the street, Tony was helping Caro sweep up the mess of gold paint chips that covered the sidewalk in front of the mission. While Angie watched, the sunbather appeared, carrying a sack of concrete mix.

"Hey! What's goin' on out here?" Chico stood behind her in the little alley.

Angie took her broom and swept it hard over the top of the picnic table. Black flies rose in the air and buzzed angrily. Then they settled back again like a solid black cloud. Chico's face looked like a black cloud, too.

"I'm sweeping," she said meekly.

"I can see that," he muttered. "Why don't you go and sweep on your own property?"

"I already did that." Angie bit her lip. Chico was no dummy. And he was proud. She decided to tell him the truth: all about Aunt Martha and trying to make things look better before Con came home.

He listened to her, and gradually he stopped frowning. But he still had a serious look on his face when he said, "Maybe your mother's right, kid. Bundy Street is kind of a slum. Nobody cares how it looks anymore."

"I care!" snapped Angie. "And so does my sister." Angie began sweeping furiously again, raising dust and flies and stale bread crumbs.

"Hey! Wait a minute, kid. You don't need to get violent about it." Chico reached out and took the broom from her. Then he began to sweep with long, powerful strokes right down to the end of the street.

When he finished, he handed her the broom and unlocked the door to Chico's. "I suppose you want me to call the sanitation department and have them clean up that mess of debris you and your sister swept into the gutters," he said.

Angie thought it over. "They might not come for a long time. Don't you think it would be better if we swept it up and put it in your big trash bins?"

Chico muttered something and disappeared. But he came back a few minutes later with a stiff-bristled push broom and several empty boxes.

When the debris filled one of Chico's bins, she and Caro leaned weakly against his counter and watched him rub his hands with soap. There were flies in here, too. Angie watched them buzz and swarm over the greasy grill like bees over honey.

Chico sighed. "They're not my fault," he insisted. "This place gets hot. You have to open the windows." Angie glanced at the open garbage bucket beside him. "OK! OK!" He put both hands out as if to stop her from looking at anything else. "I'll clean it all up. I promise. Do you want me to buy a new apron, too?"

"It would give this place a little class," Caro said.

Chico glared and shook his fist. "Git that kid outta here!" he threatened. Caro just laughed.

They walked slowly back to Flo's. Angie stopped off at the apartment to put the broom in the kitchen and a Band-Aid on a large blister on her right hand.

Her mother was heating water for instant coffee.

"Where did you get that blister?" she asked.

"Sweeping. I think Caro has one, too." Angie left the apartment before her mother could say anything else.

When she got to Flo's, she knew something had happened. Flo and Caro were standing in the kitchen of Maria's. Flo was holding a bunch of daisies wrapped in green paper with one hand, and was pointing frantically at the kitchen counter with the other.

"I must be losing my mind," she muttered. "I put them here. A whole stack of fresh tortillas. I made them early this morning, and then I went over to Old Lu's to buy some flowers for the tables. When I came back just now, they were gone."

She slapped the flowers down on the sink and put both hands on her hips. "That does it. I've heard of rats stealing food before but a whole stack of fresh tortillas is too much. That house next door is a disgrace. I'm calling the exterminators today. They can throw a tent over the top and fumigate the whole thing."

"But, Flo," Angie said, "I don't think rats even like tortillas."

"Hungry ones do. I don't want to hear anymore about it. That house is contaminated, and I'm going to see that something gets done about it."

But as soon as she got a chance, Angie went through Flo's place and checked the back door. It was standing open. Flo wasn't the kind of person to leave a door open. Angie stepped into a narrow alley that led right past the back side of the vacant house next door.

Just a few steps, and she was right next to the house. She could see why Flo was so upset about it. There was trash everywhere: old boxes and rags and even some furniture. If you wanted to get in from this side, you would have to crawl in through a window. Probably that open one, with the chair propped up beneath it. She stood there a minute, looking and listening.

She heard the same sounds she always did: the cars on the street in front; the 10:05 bus; a siren.

It was something else that had made her stop and listen. Someone was coughing, and the sound was coming from inside the old house.

Angie knew who it was. She had heard Arnold Tooker's cough before. It made her want to put her hands over her ears and run. Instead, she stood there and remembered what Jessica had said: *Took's mother is looking for him.*

Involuntarily, Angie shook herself, like a wet dog shakes off water. *So what? Let her look.* Angie was the only person who knew where he was, and she didn't intend to tell. For all she cared, Took could sit in that old house until the rats ate him.

When she got back to Flo's, she went straight through the back door and shut it behind her. She stood there shivering, as though someone had been chasing her. She was safe. She wasn't afraid of Took. So why couldn't she shake off the feeling that she still had to run?

By the end of that week, Angie could begin to see a change in Bundy Street. At first things had moved slowly. People had seemed a little embarrassed. Then they had become even more embarrassed by Angie and Caro sweeping their sidewalks for them. So they had brought out their own brooms. One thing had led to another. Now, the whole block looked cleaner, and it had begun to smell like soapy water and fresh paint.

The second week was busier. By then, no one had any excuse for not knowing what was going on. Chico saw to that. He was the best chain reactor Angie had ever seen.

"Clean up your place, or move out," he said. Then he softened the threat with, "Come on in for a cup of coffee and see how my place looks."

Angie had to hand it to him. The open garbage can disappeared, and so did his ragged apron. He even sanded down the picnic table and covered it with a coat of green enamel. There were still a few flies, but they weren't big and they didn't buzz.

Pete painted white lines on his parking lot. He had a little paint left over, so he brushed a fresh coat on Old Lu's cart. Someone at the Oak Apartments got hold of a long hose and washed down the brick face of the building. But Angie was really surprised when she went out one morning and saw that the black iron fire escape had been painted bright red.

People began to dump their cleaning water around the little trees that were planted in the sidewalk. Just as if there had been a summer rain, they sprouted new pale green growth.

But their ugly wire cages bothered Angie, and she told Tony so. "They may be for protection," she said. "But they look like prisons and collect trash."

The sunbather was on his knees patching the last piece of broken plaster in front of the mission when she said it. The next morning all the wire cages glowed with the same gold paint that covered George Washington. And when those wire cages stopped looking ugly, people stopped filling them with trash.

Corky was the only one who didn't really understand what was going on. He planted a chain-link fence around Customer Parking Only and put up a sign that said Keep Out!

Flo polished the windows of Marla's until the green plants inside showed through the glass. Then she covered the front doors of both her stores and all the window trim with bright yellow paint.

Her idea caught on, and in a few days the doors up and down Bundy Street changed colors. Blue, green, red. They looked like welcome mats hanging in the air.

It was time for welcome mats. It was Wednesday. Tomorrow morning Con was coming home.

16
HOMECOMING

Con arrived about ten o'clock in the morning. Tony went to get him and brought him home in a taxi. Everyone on Bundy Street was crowded around in front of the Deli, waiting. Everyone but Angie and her mother and Caro. They were still busy inside, getting things ready for the party. It was going to be more than a party. Bundy Street was having a real celebration.

When the taxi pulled up at the curb, Tony got out first. There was a hush, as if the whole block was holding its breath. Then Con appeared, his crutches first, and finally the rest of him, easing out of the cab, an inch at a time. Suddenly, he was standing, straight and tall, and smiling shyly.

He got a surprised look on his face. "Hey," he said as he looked slowly up and down the street. "What happened around here, anyway? Everything looks different. It ... looks great!"

Bundy Street let out its breath, breathed in again, and cheered. Everybody kept clapping and yelling while he walked slowly across the sidewalk and stood in the doorway of the Deli.

"I ... want to thank everybody," he said. "You were all really good to me when ... I was sick." Then Con leaned one of his crutches against the wall and lifted one arm. It was like a kind of salute.

Angie could only see his back from where she stood inside the store. But she saw that he held himself straight and tall. Then he turned, with both crutches under his arms, and saw her.

"Hi," he said softly.

"Hi, yourself," she whispered back.

For a second it seemed like they were the only two people in the room. Angie wondered how she could have forgotten that when Con was happy his eyes seemed full of sky.

Then there were people everywhere, talking to Con and patting him on the back and helping themselves to hot tamales and pastrami sandwiches. Con sat on a stool and talked to everybody. On the counter in front of him was Flo's vase with one single, fresh flower. Angie had brought it from the hospital the night before and filled it early this morning.

After a while Tony went to the back room and brought out a large sheet cake. It was chocolate inside and out, but the letters that said Welcome Home, Con, were as yellow as sunshine.

Con cut the cake himself, and passed the first piece to Angie. Tony put his arm around her, but he was looking at her mother when he spoke.

"We're all together today," he said.

Con shook his head. "All but one. Does anybody know what happened to Took?"

Angie put her cake down without tasting it. She hadn't eaten much all day, and she still wasn't hungry.

"What's the matter, Angie? You look funny." Caro edged up closer. "Aren't you going to eat your cake?"

Angie shook her head. "You eat it. I'm ... I guess I'm too excited to eat." She turned to listen to Flo, who was telling about her tortilla mystery.

"The whole stack was gone," Flo insisted. "A stack of tortillas doesn't just walk off by itself."

Tony laughed. "Well, Flo, those rats you've been telling us about must be strong ones, because I missed a few things around here this week myself. One of them was half a gallon of milk. If a rat managed to carry that off, I'll ..."

"I've been missing things, too." Chico had joined the group. "Listen, Flo. I think it's just some kid."

"Rats!" Flo insisted. "But you don't have to worry about them, because I know where they're coming from, and I've already taken care of it."

Everybody stopped talking and looked at her. She nodded vigorously. "I called the health department about that house, and they called the owner. It seems that he's trying to sell the place, but it has termites. The exterminators are coming early tomorrow morning. By the time they cover the place with plastic and spray poisonous gas inside, nothing that lives there will have a chance."

Angie swallowed. *Took lives there, Flo. I heard him cough. He's hiding inside that house.*

She picked up a paper cup full of punch and pretended to take a drink. Took would just have to find someplace else to hide. In the morning when the exterminators came, he would hear them, and he'd get out.

But what if he didn't? What if he was asleep and didn't wake up in time? What if he was sick? Angie tried to keep her mind from visualizing the plastic tent that would cover the old house. It would be sealed off. No air could get in.

It's none of my business! Arnold Tooker isn't my responsibility. Anyway, I didn't actually see him. I only heard somebody cough.

Angie jumped when Con reached out and touched her hand. "Hey," he said and placed one finger on the tip of her nose. "How about it?"

She knew what he meant, and she forced herself to smile back at him. It was their old secret, their signal for a smile that said, "I'm OK ... you're OK."

But Angie wasn't OK. Her skin felt hot, and her throat was dry. The sight of all that food made her sick. It wasn't fair. She shouldn't have to think about Took. She wasn't his keeper.

For the rest of the day she concentrated on keeping Took out of her mind. She talked to Con, and worked at Flo's, and talked to Con some more. Then she went home to lie down, because her head ached, and she felt heavy and tired all over.

She lay in the apartment, pretending to sleep, while her mother got ready and left for work. Caro came by and looked at her a couple of times. Angie recognized her footsteps. But Angie didn't move. She didn't want to talk to anybody or do anything. She just wanted to lie there with an empty head.

That was the trouble. Her head wouldn't stay empty. No matter how hard she tried, Angie couldn't stop thinking about tomorrow morning, and that meant she had to think about Took.

She opened her eyes and sat up. She felt terrible, and it was all his fault. He had no right to hide in that awful place or steal food or cough so that she could hear him. Besides that, he had ruined Con's homecoming. At least, he had ruined it for her.

Angie stood up. She was going to the old house. She was going to find Took and tell him about tomorrow morning. She also intended to tell him exactly what she thought of him.

Angie smiled. She felt better already. Arnold Tooker wasn't going to be on her conscience. As soon as he left the old house, she would be rid of him forever. She went out the front door and tried not to think about the rats.

It was early evening on Bundy Street. The sky was still light, but the sun had dropped low behind the buildings of West Los Angeles, and long shadows darkened the sidewalks and cooled the warm July air.

Angie walked quickly. She didn't want anyone to see where she was going. This was private business—between her and Took.

She walked as quietly as she could, but she wasn't sure why. People always walked quietly, she realized, when they weren't quite sure what they'd find.

But she found things just the way she had seen them two weeks ago. Boxes of trash and old furniture were still piled up against the house. Debris was still scattered on the ground.

Angie stopped and listened. She didn't hear anything from the inside. Maybe Took had already gone. But that didn't help Angie. She had to know for sure.

She went to the side of the house next to Second Chance, where the chair was still propped under the open window. When Angie tried it, it seemed to hold her weight. She put both hands on the windowsill and pulled herself up.

The opening was wide enough, but the window was stuck tight, halfway open, so that she had to either go through headfirst on her stomach or sideways, one leg at a time. She decided she would rather meet a rat with her foot than with her face, and swung one leg over the sill, crouching low, so her head would miss the window. She felt for a foothold and found it. Then she eased herself into the room and stood, motionless, waiting for the pulse to stop pounding in her throat.

The house wasn't empty. It was full of dark shadows and shapes. Whoever had lived there had left a lot of stuff behind them. Mostly junk, like the broken bed in the corner and the box of books with the pages half eaten by rats. Angie moved forward cautiously. On a table was a candle, stuck in a pool of melted wax, a package of matches that said Maria's, and what looked like part of a sandwich. Angie poked at it with the back of one finger. It was a piece of rolled-up tortilla, and it was as hard and dry as a stale crust of bread.

She heard something from another part of the house. A click. Like the sound of a door being carefully closed. Then she heard another sound. She couldn't be sure, but Angie thought someone was coughing.

She shivered and rubbed both arms with the palms of her hands. She must be out of her mind. How could she be so sure it was Took she had heard that day? Anyone could be hiding in a place like this. She was a fool to be in here alone; it was getting darker all the time.

"Took?" She called his name softly and tiptoed across the room to a door that opened onto a central hallway. "Took?" Her voice was almost a whisper.

Something furry brushed against the side of her foot and scurried across the floor. Two bright eyes shone against the darkness at the back of the hall. Angie could see the shape of its body and the curved tail.

Angie shuddered and hugged herself. Horrible little creature. Did rats bite? She was almost sure they did. She backed slowly along the wall until she came to another doorway on the opposite side of the hall. It was open, and she went in.

Angie couldn't see as well in here. A dark blind covered the only window, and almost no light came in from the hall. And it was dirty. It smelled old and stale— and fearful.

"Took!" She said his name firmly. Her voice had a hollow sound in the empty room. She felt like she was speaking to the air. "Took, listen. It's me. Angie."

Nothing happened. Angie stood absolutely still and strained her ears to catch the slightest sound. She listened so hard, she almost felt that she could hear the old house breathing. She did hear the sound of breathing! Heavy and strained, like it was being pumped through too small a hole. In and out, in and out. Then she heard the other sound. A painful, hacking cough that always ended with a wheeze and could belong to only one person.

"Took!" Angie said his name louder. "Took, I know you're here. I'm not leaving until I talk to you."

She walked across the room to the closet door and put her hand on the knob. This was what she had been waiting for. Took was on the other side of that door, and she was ready for him.

For an instant her mind zeroed in on his image. If it hadn't been for Took, Angie was sure all her dreams would still be intact. He was the reason for everything bad that had happened to her. She took a deep breath. Once Arnold Tooker was out of her life, Angie was sure she would be OK. She turned the knob and opened the door.

He sat huddled on the floor of the empty closet with his back curled into the corner and his legs doubled underneath him. One candle stood in a chipped dish on the floor. It was burning, and he kept holding his hands out over the flame as if he needed to warm them. Angie saw that his hands were shaking. So was the rest of him.

"Took," she whispered. "What's wrong?"

"Close the door!" He wheezed loudly, trying to get his breath, and made urgent beckoning motions with both hands. "Quick! Quick! Close it so they won't get in!"

They must be the rats. Angie remembered wishing once that the rats would get him. But now that she'd seen one, she wasn't sure she would wish that on anybody. Not even Took.

She slipped quickly into the closet and pulled the door shut behind her. It was awful in there. Took looked sick and smelled dirty, and the candle was one of those cheap scented ones that made you nauseated if you smelled it very long.

He rested his head against the wall and rubbed his hands together over the candle. Then he began to cough. His face screwed up as if he were in pain, and he held one dirty hand around his throat and tried to get his breath.

"Hey, Took." She reached over and touched him on the shoulder just like she had poked at the stale tortilla in the other room. "Hey, Took. I've got to tell you something."

He lifted his head slowly, and he looked at Angie as if he had never seen her before. Caro had looked like that once when she was really sick and had a high fever. Delirious. That's what her mother had called it, and that was what Took acted like right now.

"Took. You've got to listen to me. This is really important. They're going to fumigate this place in the morning, and you have to get out."

Took lowered his head and began to cough. "Cold …" He shivered. "I'm awful cold."

Angie sighed. He was the most exasperating person she had ever known. She had gone to a lot of trouble, and he wasn't even listening.

"Took! Look at me. It's Angie."

"Angie?" He pulled back away from her as if someone had threatened him. His eyes weren't Took's eyes at all. The old sly look that had always made her want to look the other way was gone. He reminded Angie of a small, trapped animal that was too weak to fight.

"Don't hurt me," he whimpered. He put up one hand as if to keep her away. "I didn't mean it. Honest, Angie. I only wanted …" He began to cough. His eyes closed, and he shivered violently.

Angie shivered, too. He looked really sick. She got down on her knees and put one hand on his forehead. His skin was hot and dry. She couldn't believe how hot it was. He was making so much noise breathing that she could hardly catch his next words.

"I ... lied, Angie. Accident ... my fault. Con ... was ... was trying to save ... me." He took a deep breath and began to cry. There weren't any tears, just dry, racking sobs that filled his throat and made him cough harder. "I'm ... sorry. I'm so sorry. I wish I was ... dead."

Suddenly, he was silent. His eyes closed, and his coughing stopped, and the only sound in the closet was the sound of his strangled breathing.

The candle flickered. In a few moments it would go out. Angie closed her eyes and leaned her head against the wall. She thought how good it would feel to put her head on a pillow in her own bed with clean, cool sheets covering her.

But she wasn't at home. She was in a dark closet with Took. She felt all tight inside, just the way she had felt that night on the roof when she had asked for help and it hadn't come. It wasn't coming now, either.

If you're my father, why won't you show me what to do? Why are you always putting me behind a closed door and keeping me there?

Angie had never felt so frustrated in her life. It seemed like everything she had planned to do had drained out of her and left her empty inside. She looked at Took, huddled miserably in his dark corner. She couldn't leave him.

His eyes flicked open. "... scared, Angie. I'm so scared. Please don't hurt me."

She pulled back as if she had been burned. But what he said was true, wasn't it? She had wanted to hurt him. He was obnoxious, dirty, rude. He lied and cheated, and she hated him. Now here she was, sitting with him on the floor. She was the only one who could save him.

She reached out and touched his hand. "I won't hurt you, Took. I'm telling you the truth. Nobody's going to hurt you." Angie looked at him and was surprised. She saw a human being.

She took a deep breath. Even in the rancid air of the

closet, it seemed to go all the way to her fingertips. She got up on her feet. The closet door was still closed, but it wasn't locked. She could open it and walk out whenever she was ready. But she had to bring Arnold Tooker out with her.

She pulled at his hand. "Come on, Took. Let's get out of here."

He wasn't much help. He was sick and weak, and he was afraid of the rats. He mumbled and protested and kicked over the candle so that there wasn't any light at all. Angie had to fumble until she found the doorknob.

She half dragged, half carried him into the hall. She knew she could never get him through that window at the back of the house. There was only one way out. She hooked Took's left arm over her shoulder and her right arm around his waist. He wasn't very heavy. She was surprised how easy it was to take him all the way to the front door. Angie slipped the bolt and turned the knob.

It was past twilight on Bundy Street. The streetlamp on the corner sent a ring of yellow light through the warm summer air. A golden ring, Angie thought, reaching out and wrapping around them both.

"Come on, Took. It's only a little farther," she said. "I'm taking you home."

17
CATCH A GOLDEN RING

Angie's mother took one look at Took and got him to the hospital as fast as she could. Tony went with her in a taxi, and they were gone for a long time.

Angie and Con waited on the front porch of the apartment building. Caro was with them, but she was asleep, with her head in Angie's lap. Con leaned his crutches against the railing and eased himself onto the top step, and that's where he stayed. Angie was sure he was uncomfortable and tired after the long day.

Finally they saw Tony and Angie's mother coming along the sidewalk. They were walking close together. Angie caught her breath.

Angie's mother looked a little flustered. Her cheeks were pink, and Angie didn't think it was because of the walk from the hospital. Tony looked fine. His shoulders were back, and his head was high.

"Took is going to be OK," he told them. "But it's a good thing Angie found him when she did. He has pneumonia, and he'll have to stay in the hospital for several days. That boy really did a pretty good job of hiding, didn't he? I guess he felt so guilty about Con's accident that he couldn't face anybody, not even his own mother."

Angie had forgotten all about Took's mother. "She's

been looking for him," she said. "Jessica's the one who told me. She said that Took's mother is about ready to call the police." Then, as if to herself, "I didn't even know that Took had a mother. But Jessica did. She must have talked to her."

Tony nodded. "She probably did. Jessica and Took are cousins, Angie."

Angie's mouth dropped open. "Cousins! You mean Jessica Smith is related to Took?"

Tony nodded again. "Sometimes," he told her, "it's a smaller world than we think it is." He stopped and frowned. "I don't know exactly where Old Lu lives, but she's always on her corner bright and early. I'll tell her about Took in the morning."

"Old Lu?"

"I guess not too many people know about that," Tony told them. "Took was always pretty much on his own, but Old Lu is his mother just the same. She's really not so old. I think she makes a pretty decent living selling her flowers, but she hasn't made much of a home for her son."

Angie looked at her own mother. She was young looking and pretty, and Angie loved her, even if she did want to send them to Aunt Martha's. "What's going to happen to Took now?" she asked. "After he gets out of the hospital, I mean."

"That's something else we'll have to think about later," Tony told her. "I understand the new owners of the old house on the corner are willing to rent it pretty cheap. It might make a nice flower shop."

Con was shaking his head back and forth. "I still can't believe it," he said. "Jessica is Took's cousin. Took never mentioned it. He never mentioned Old Lu either, but, now that I think about it, he used to hang around her corner a lot."

Angie nodded. "I noticed that, too. Once I saw her give him some money, but I thought she was just feeling sorry for him. How could his own mother let him disappear and not do anything ..."

"Angie." Tony's voice was gentle. "You never know what's on the inside of another person. We all have our secrets." He yawned and put his arm gently around Angie's mother. "Right now, I think we had better call it a day." He helped Con to his feet and handed him his crutches, and they started off across the street.

Angie and her mother half carried Caro into the apartment and put her to bed. Then they stood a minute, just looking at each other. Angie was thinking about what she had seen a few minutes before: her mother and Tony, so happy together.

"Mom ... about the other night. You know, when I heard you talking about Caro and me living with Aunt Martha? Well, I've been thinking. If you want us to go there, I guess we can stand it."

Her mother reached for her. "Oh, Angie, honey. I never mailed the letter. Tony was right. Families should be together. Anyway, I couldn't stand the thought of sending you girls away." She looked thoughtful. "The last two weeks have been eye-openers, Angie. Bundy Street is changing."

Angie hugged her mother. Inside, she felt like a jig-saw puzzle that was finally being put back together again. A lot of the picture was still missing, but at least all the pieces were on the table.

Then her mother pulled away a little, and Angie saw that her face was pink, just like it had been outside. "I ... have something important to tell you, Angie. Tony and I ... That is, you do like Tony, don't you, Angie?"

Angie laughed out loud. She laughed so loud that Caro opened her eyes and sat up in the bed.

Like Tony? Tony was so special, she didn't even have the right words to tell how she felt. But she did the best she could. "After Con," she told her mother, "Tony Genovese is my best friend."

"Then you won't mind if he's your stepfather? If we all live at the Deli together? There's plenty of room in the back. I'm sure we can ..."

Angie didn't even let her finish. "You and Tony and Con and Caro and me ... and Bandit, too? We'll be the mixed-up family of Bundy Street!"

Caro lay back in the bed and closed her eyes. But she only pulled the covers up as far as her chin.

Angie had trouble sleeping that night. So much had happened. It all seemed to be floating around in her head like a giant traffic jam.

Finally, when it was almost daylight, she unlocked the apartment door, slipped the key into her pocket, and quietly went outside and stood on the front porch.

Bundy Street was quiet now, as if it were resting. In a little while, the sun would come up, and cars would move noisily along the street. Old Lu would take her place on the corner. Chico would sweep away yesterday's crumbs. Flo would plug in the big pot of coffee and start frying fresh tortillas on the hot grill. Con would open his eyes and know he was home.

A lot of it was the same, but at the same time everything was different. Bundy Street wasn't just a run-down block on the city's west side. It was made of people. They could laugh, and they could cry, and Angie knew now that they could care about each other.

Bundy Street would always be a part of her life. She knew it, and she didn't mind anymore. Because the sign over the mission was true after all. Prayer did change things. When you talked to God, he showed you how to grow. He was just like a father, leading you and guiding you and loving you, even when you were wrong.

That's exactly what had happened to her. God had led her like a father would, letting her know, down inside, what it was she had to do. It had started back on the roof when she had asked for help and didn't know it was already starting to come. He had shown her a light flickering in the old house. He had led her straight to Took. He had shown her how to unlock the door for another human being. He had spoken to her in feelings instead of words. Even when she tried to turn and run the other way, he had led her, pointed her, prodded her, until finally she had to look her enemy in the face. And it wasn't Took at all. It was the bad feeling about him that lived inside of her.

She raised her eyes to the eastern sky, all blue and purple and pink and yellow. The sun came up every morning, Angie thought, and it went down again every night. It was something you could depend on.

Tony called it opportunity. Mr. Erickson called it faith. But Angie knew what it really was. A promise. It was the future, all wrapped up in golden ribbon. God's gift to his children.

Angie saw the climbing vine that she had called a weed. It was covered with blue flowers, opening wide and spreading their faces toward the rising sun—just as if they had been waiting to catch a golden ring of light.

Catching a golden ring, Angie thought, was seeing a morning glory grow out of a crack in the sidewalk and bloom. It was listening to Tony Genovese's gypsy music and feeling like a whisper on the wind. It was starting a chain reaction from one end of Bundy Street to the other. It was forgiving and being forgiven, understanding and being understood.

But just because you help somebody, just because you feel a responsibility, doesn't mean you own them. You have to let the people you love go free. Angie supposed that was the way God felt, too. He let you make your own decisions. Otherwise, you'd be just like Bandit, with a rope around your neck.

At last she got up and went into the house. She had a lot of plans to make. First, she was going to see Con, just so she could tell herself he was really home. Then she was going down the street to buy a flower for Took.

In the afternoon, she was going to keep a promise she had made a long time ago. This was the day she was going to take Caro to La Mirada Beach.

She remembered how she'd felt that time with Con when she had ridden on the carousel for the first time. She had been kind of afraid to try. But she had taken a chance, leaned out and stretched herself farther than she thought she could. She had touched the golden ring, felt it slip away, reached out again, and then she had finally held it in her hand.

She held it now. But not in her hand. It was deep inside her, like a warm glow. She smiled to herself. She could imagine what Caro would say when she saw the merry-go-round.

"I can't catch the golden ring, Angie. My arms are too short."

But Angie would help her. She would have lots of time to show Caro that you don't have to have long arms to catch a golden ring. You reach out for it with your heart.

UNITED CHURCH OF CHRIST
963 LAUREL AVENUE
BRIDGEPORT, CONN. 06604